THREE SCENARIOS IN WHICH
HANA SASAKI GROWS A TAIL

THREE
SCENARIOS
IN WHICH
HANA SASAKI
GROWS A TAIL

BY KELLY LUCE

A
STRANGE
OBJECT
Austin, Texas

STORIES

The stories in this collection have appeared in slightly different form in the following journals:

"Ms. Yamada's Toaster" in *Tampa Review* and *Storyville*, "The Blue Demon of Ikumi" in *Salamander*, "Reunion" in the *Kenyon Review*, "Rooey" in the *Literary Review*, "Pioneers" in *Kyoto Journal* (under the title "A Sort of Deadline"), "Three Scenarios in Which Hana Sasaki Grows a Tail" in *Shenandoah*, "Wisher" in the *Southern Review*, "Ash" in the *Gettysburg Review*, "Cram Island" in *Kartika Review*, and "Amorometer" in *Crazyhorse*.

"Ms. Yamada's Toaster" was also featured in the anthology *Tomo: Friendship through Fiction* (Stone Bridge Press, 2012).

Published by
A Strange Object
astrangeobject.com

ISBN 978-0-9892759-1-0

Cover illustration by Yuko Shimizu
Cover design by Eric Amling
Book design by Amber Morena

For my mom

CONTENTS

鰯の頭も信心から

(Iwashi no kashira mo shinjin kara.)

Belief delivers power to even the sardine's head.

秋茄子は嫁に食わすな

(Akinasu wa yome ni kuwasuna.)

Don't let your daughter-in-law eat your autumn eggplants.

MS. YAMADA'S TOASTER
\\\\\\\\\

AT THE TIME, MY UNCLE OWNED the liquor store and I delivered bottles for him on Mondays, then went back on Fridays and picked up the empties. In this way I got to know the whole town. Pretty much everyone did business with my uncle at one point or another.

Even though I was only fourteen, he let me drive his delivery truck. The hills in town were too steep for a bike; plus, I had to carry around all those bottles.

Old Kumo lived in a shack behind the temple and was brown and furrowed like an old piece of fruit. We kids called him Hoshi-sumomo-san, Mr. Prune, though I never knew whether this referred to his appearance or his diet.

It was from Old Kumo that I first heard about Ms. Yamada's toaster and how it could predict the way a person's going to die. I was setting the bottles on his mossy concrete step when he appeared in the doorway and said in a voice as wrinkled as his face, "Son, today I learned how I'm gonna go."

I had finished with the bottles and stood there, unsure of what to say. I looked up at him because, even though it's rude to look your elders right in the eye like that, it seemed to be what he wanted.

He told me Ms. Yamada had a toaster that when you put in a piece of bread, it came out with a kanji character toasted on it. That character indicated how you'd die.

"What was your word, sir?"

"Sleep. Isn't that a hoot? Now I can finally live in peace." He waved as he shuffled back inside, a bottle of sake clutched in his left hand.

I DIDN'T TELL ANYONE AT HOME what Old Kumo had said. My parents were too busy—that was the year they opened the udon restaurant—and my sister had just gotten a boyfriend and never hung around after school anymore. Plus, I had a feeling no one would care. Mine was a family of skeptics. We didn't observe any superstitious holidays, bean-throwing day or Tanabata or anything like that; all we celebrated was New Year's and that's because you get to feast for three days straight.

I picked up Old Kumo's empties on Friday and brought him two extra bottles of sake, which he'd special-ordered that week. On Monday he was dead. Died in his sleep of natural causes.

Apparently Old Kumo had told a lot of people about Ms. Yamada's toaster and its prediction for him, though, because once he died, everyone in town was talking about it. Ms. Yamada had always been a little weird. She confirmed everything: the toaster had predicted her husband's death last year when it popped out a piece of bread that read "heart" three days before he had a coronary, and after that it had foretold her mother-in-law's fatal pneumonia. A gift from God, she told the crowd gathered around her at the market. She held the toaster under one arm, its plug swinging beneath it like a tail. When asked if she'd gotten a death-predicting piece of toast herself, she said she had.

"Well?"

Hers had read "cancer." It was quiet for a while after that.

MS. YAMADA WAS JUST LIKE any other lady you'd see around town except for one thing—she was a real religious nut. Years before the toaster, she'd knocked on our door a couple times, offering her "help." I remember thinking it was kind of nice—weird, but nice—but after she'd gone my mom would roll her eyes and go back to her TV drama. Anyway, that was back when I was little. By the time the toaster came around, Ms. Yamada didn't knock in our neighborhood anymore.

Her house was at the edge of town, partway up a huge,

terraced hill with bamboo at the top. For a widow living alone, she had a pretty big standing order at my uncle's store—eight tall one-liter bottles of beer. That was more than a liter a day! She who smelled so sweet it hurt your nose, like overripe peaches, and spoke very properly and always wore something with lace on the collar—how could *she* go through that much beer?

I thought of her at her impeccable kitchen table, pouring the beer into a glass and waiting patiently for it to settle, then taking the tiniest sip. I pictured her melting at the first drop of bitter liquid in her throat, her creamy makeup running down her neck, pooling between her breasts and in her belly button, and the starch on her collar drooping until her whole body oozed into a peach-scented puddle of foam.

THE TOASTER BECAME A SENSATION. Some people thought it was a trick she was using to try and convert people, while others believed in the toaster's power but disagreed about what ought to be done with it. Some wanted to enshrine the toaster and worship it like a Shinto deity. Others thought she should sell it to the government.

But the thing people argued about most was whether or not it was right to use the toaster's powers, to become One Who Knew. Soon the town divided itself between Knows and Didn't-Want-To-Knows. Each group, of course, claimed the moral high ground—there was no room for compromise. Conflicting opinions on the topic spoiled countless friendships and were even named in the

Satos' divorce proceedings as evidence of irreconcilable differences.

Ms. Yamada didn't get involved in the politics of it. She let anyone use the toaster. She believed it was a gift from God that should not go to waste. Every day there was a line out her door of people, soft pieces of white bread in hand, hoping to find out in what fashion they would meet Death.

But some of the Didn't-Want-To-Knows were upset. One man, a retired professor from Keio University who everyone just called "Mr. Doc," went so far as to stand at Ms. Yamada's open door and protest. He was there talking quietly and intently to a young mother and her toddler on the front steps when I came the next Friday to pick up Ms. Yamada's empties. They paid no attention to me as I stepped past and set the bottles in the entranceway. I could hear someone crying in the kitchen.

On the way out I passed the mother and child, who were walking toward the road with Mr. Doc. I guess he'd convinced her not to go in. I kept my head down, but as I passed he called to me.

"Keisuke."

I turned, stunned he knew my name.

"Are you planning to find out?"

I shrugged. It seemed like an awfully big thing to know. Plus I kind of liked thinking that maybe I'd never die, like by the time I got old they'd have invented a cure for everything.

"I'm fighting a losing battle," he said. "You just can't protect people from themselves."

I bowed and walked quickly back to the truck. On the drive down I passed four groups of people climbing the hill to Ms. Yamada's house. I wondered if Mr. Doc would be able to stop all of them.

BY MONDAY EVERY HOUSE I VISITED buzzed with talk of the toaster. Ms. Kawabata was predicted to die by fire—the same as Ms. Shinjo. Both were librarians. Extra fire extinguishers were purchased for the older wooden library building, and a state-of-the-art sprinkler system was installed.

A newlywed couple canceled their honeymoon flight to Hawaii because both of their pieces of toast had popped up bearing the character "air."

At dinnertime my parents and sister talked about how nuts everyone was, but I kept quiet. I didn't necessarily believe in the toaster, but I was at least willing to be convinced, maybe.

The news reached all over the prefecture. The line spilled out Ms. Yamada's door and down the steps. News vans crowded the narrow street so that I had to drive fifty meters away to park.

Mr. Doc held forth on the front stoop. "Don't let curiosity pollute your mind!" he bellowed at the line, which was full of unfamiliar faces. A few college-age kids stood with him, holding signs and chanting, "Knowledge of death sullies the will to live!" The crowd ignored them and was silent, as if in line to receive a blessing. I stepped through the mob with the beer, excusing myself and sneaking peeks at the faces. Some people seemed lost in thought, staring up at the bamboo grove beyond the house, while others whispered nervously to one another.

"Hey, no cuts, buddy," someone said as I passed. I held up the crate of beer and almost said, "Delivery," but then I thought that maybe Ms. Yamada didn't want these people to know she'd ordered all this beer, so I turned back.

I lingered near my truck and watched people come down the stairs, each clutching a piece of toast. So many People Who Knew. Some looked confused and some relieved. One woman was bawling so hard she dropped her toast, and when she did, I saw what it said: *suicide*.

That was eerie, but even eerier were the ones whose faces were blank and empty and lost. Like maybe they were already dead.

A cry rose from the front of the crowd, and suddenly everyone got very noisy. People gestured and talked amongst themselves, and some turned away and started heading back toward the road.

"Broken? Right! I *knew* it was a fraud."

"Just my luck . . . should've come earlier."

"Not really sure I wanted to know, to be honest . . ."

I waited until everyone left, then approached the door with my crate.

"Yamada-san?"

She stepped into the hall, prim as ever.

"Keisuke! How good of you to come amid that throng. I noticed the truck outside earlier and thought you'd given up."

"No, ma'am." I held the crate out, and she took it without a word. I shifted around, trying to sneak a peek into the kitchen.

"Come on in and have a drink," she said.

There it was, unplugged, sitting right smack in the middle of the round yellow table, a silver single-slice toaster trimmed in black, with rust lining the opening. The table was littered with crumbs. I wondered if you had to eat the toast in order for the prediction to come true, or if just toasting it was enough.

"Well, there it is."

"Is it . . . broken?" I asked.

She frowned. "Seems to be."

"Did it really work, though?"

Her smile returned, serene above her lace collar. "Oh, yes! God's methods sure are beyond our comprehension. Who are we to judge His ways?"

"But . . . maybe you can get it fixed."

"Maybe. But perhaps this is simply the toaster's fate."

She took a bottle from the crate and gestured with it toward the back door. "Please, come."

I FOLLOWED HER OUT THE BACK DOOR. The yard had been completely overtaken by a junglelike garden that seemed out of step with Ms. Yamada's tidy appearance and manners. We picked through vines until we reached the back of the yard, where a stone shrine stood against the first tall mud terrace. The family grave.

"This is where my ancestors rest, and most recently, my husband," she said, picking up the bottle opener lying at the base of the shrine.

"He loved beer. His favorite thing in life was a cold beer in the garden at sunset. Ah, Shuji," she said.

She opened the beer deftly and poured it all over the shrine, slowly dousing the statuary in caramel foam. She shook the bottle wildly at the end, spraying us both with drops of beer. She looked like my sister dancing to a Morning Musume song when she did that.

When the bottle was dry, she set it on the ledge where offerings are left. The family name, Yamada—heavenly mountain and earthly rice field—was carved in fancy calligraphy above the shelf, and beer meandered down the grooves in the stone like a lazy river in summer.

She sighed. "I do that every day. That is my offering to him."

After what I'd just witnessed, I felt comfortable enough to ask, "Yamada-san, what about the eighth bottle?"

She laughed. "You are an astute fellow."

SHE WENT IN THE HOUSE and returned with the toaster and another bottle.

"Do you know what baptism is?"

"No, Yamada-san."

"Baptism is a ritual that washes away original sin," she said, setting the toaster on the offering ledge. She reached again for the opener. "It makes you pure."

Then she held the bottle over her head, closed her eyes, and turned it upside down.

I reached out automatically to help her, to save her from herself, but she raised her palm. The beer gushed over her hair, her face, onto her white, starched shirt and long, beige skirt. Her hair flattened out. Here and there her makeup ran off her cheeks and revealed darker skin underneath.

About three-quarters through she stopped, opened her eyes, and held the bottle out to me.

I didn't move. All I could hear was the drip-drip-drip of beer hitting the dirt around Ms. Yamada's feet. I know what my uncle would've said: what a waste of alcohol. He always said it was a sin to waste liquor.

My impulse was to take the bottle—maybe she wanted me to hold it for her—but then she raised it to the sky and said, "For once, they came to me. I did the best I could, I explained God's true will and purpose, and how to be saved, but no one listened."

The remaining beer sloshed around inside the bottle. Her eyes were closed. It seemed she'd forgotten I was standing there.

"I have brought no one into the truth," she said.

She opened her eyes and looked around, teetering as if she'd drunk all that beer instead of showering in it. When she noticed I was still there, she held the bottle out to me once again. Strands of wet hair clung to her cheeks. She smiled a smile I've never forgotten, a smile like a girl playing in a puddle.

I stepped close to her, close enough so that I could see the pink brassiere through her damp blouse. Together we emptied the bottle into the toaster's vacant slot. When the slot overflowed, she pushed down the lever on the side.

She looked toward the sky. I wondered if she was thinking of her own death.

I followed her gaze. I could see the hilltop behind us, and the bamboo growing there. The stalks moved slightly in a breeze I couldn't feel, revealing and concealing slivers of blue that formed words faster than I could read them, a marvel for anyone who cared to look.

THE BLUE DEMON OF IKUMI
\\\\\\\\\

MASA UNLATCHED THE GRIMY WINDOW. A seaweed breeze doused the room, flushing out the smell of air freshener. On the low table, silk flowers stood in a vase of water. Saki sat before the table, popping off the petals so only the plastic stems remained.

"Let's stay forever," she said while Masa arranged their suitcases against the wall. There was no closet.

Masa had picked this inn on purpose—cheap and tacky, exactly the kind of place Saki loved. It hadn't been his first choice for a honeymoon destination, of course, but he wanted Saki happy, wanted her, more than anything, to feel *known*; his first wife had complained Masa didn't understand her, or want to. And maybe that was true. He worked too much in those days; he was younger, still selfish.

Having denuded all the silk stems, Saki lay back and began to curl in and out of slow sit-ups. "I've decided to cultivate a twelve-pack," she said. "My wedding gift to you."

Masa leaned against the wall, admiring his wife. He'd first encountered her less than a year ago in an Osaka art gallery. She'd been hunkered on the floor before a toe-tapping marionette, wearing a print dress with a rip in the hem. Her long hair was unbrushed, and the soles had separated from her tennis shoes. She wore no makeup. Masa liked this. He'd just turned fifty and didn't need the worry of handling a beauty.

"Saki-chan, shall we stroll on the beach?" he said. He had something important to discuss, and had found serious conversations were best held while engaging in simple, physical activity. "I bet this typhoon washed up some interesting things."

She rolled gracefully to her feet. "You know I love debris."

ALONG THE EDGES OF THE COVE, concrete bulwarks rose from the water like ancient creatures. The sky was flat and gray, silver water meeting a dark horizon. Clumps of seaweed ringed the shore. The air smelled of fish, but the breeze tasted faintly sweet, like ice cream. Masa felt content; this was not something he would have noticed before meeting Saki.

Now that they were married, it was time to discuss something of utmost importance: starting a family. It was a topic they'd addressed only indirectly—things had happened so fast—but Masa knew, the same way he knew that she'd love this crumbling inn, that Saki wanted children. Yes, she was unpredictable, nontraditional, even a bit eccentric, but she was still a woman. Kaori had wanted kids so badly she'd secretly stopped taking her birth control pills. When she got pregnant, they got married, and when she miscarried, he felt cheated, like an animal lured into a cage.

But that was all in the past.

He caught Saki's hand in his. He gave it a squeeze and cleared his throat.

Just then they came upon the body of a gull lying in a bed of bright green seaweed. One eye was open, fixing them with its orange iris. Masa led Saki on, but she resisted.

"Poor thing," she said. "How does a bird drown?"

"We don't know it did. Maybe it died on land and was swept away."

"Or maybe it got blown off course by the typhoon. Just imagine. Flying and flying but nowhere to land, and you're so tired . . ."

"Surely it was already dead," he said firmly, annoyed that he would have to put off their discussion now that such a bad omen had presented itself.

"Maybe you're right. I bet it lived a full life, flying where it pleased." Saki gazed at him behind the hair blown across her face. She jumped with both feet into the tide as it came in, her long toes leaving tiny prints that melted as he watched.

They walked on, the damp, packed sand whining beneath their feet until they stood at the end of the beach, where a stone slab rose from a pile of rubble. Words had been carved into the rock—thin, shallow cuts.

"'In great reverence . . .'" Masa read slowly. "I don't even recognize some of those characters, they're so old."

Saki reached toward the stone and laid two fingers on the characters carved there.

"'In deep appreciation for the gift from the sea . . . in this the year of . . .'" She pointed to a character whose strokes blended together.

"I think this is the old character for *blue*. Or more like the . . . *essence of blue*," Saki said.

Masa loved her way with the Japanese language. She used the old words for things, *o-hia* for water, *seppun* instead of the modern *kisu* when she wanted a kiss.

He thought of his mother, full of warnings about marrying a *hafu*—a girl only half Japanese. And, she'd added wryly, practically half his age. How stubborn the old woman could be.

He made up his mind. Barring another bad omen, he would bring up children at dinner.

THINGS WERE GOING WELL. Saki's puppetry career was coming along, though she went through more money than she brought in. Still, though, the finances were more than stable, thanks to a couple clever property investments Masa had made after his divorce. It was the right time to take the next step; Masa felt it in his bones.

That night, they walked down the empty main street to the town's other, fancier hotel, which had a restaurant with a medieval theme. They sat in over-large chairs; his upholstered in leather, hers in dark animal fur. Over dinner, Saki leaned in close. "I can tell you want to talk. I'm all ears," she said, and grabbed her earlobes.

Masa felt a rush of love for her, for that face like a heart, for those gray eyes that, when focused on him, held so much light.

He reached forward and encircled her wrists with two fingers. "I—I want to have a baby." There, he had said it; not the eloquent speech he had practiced, but then again Saki was his wife, not a client.

"Now?"

"Yes. I'm—well, I'm no grandpa, but I'm not shedding years, either."

"It's possible, maybe in a few years. After my career has developed."

"Even now, you could still pursue your art. Sometimes—well, sometimes fate has other things planned."

"You and your fate."

She wasn't at all superstitious; in fact, she went out of her way to be unlucky. When Masa's mother express-mailed them a Shinto calendar to use in selecting a wedding date, Saki picked the least auspicious day of the year. His mother had refused to come to the ceremony.

In fact, Masa hadn't talked to his mother since the calendar incident. His father made a point of calling one Sunday a month, but he rarely asked about Saki and never used her name; it was always, "and did She accompany you on that trip?" or "how is Her health?" Saki found it funny. "I'm your lawfully wedded pronoun," she said.

"Everything about us is fate," Masa said. "It's all meant to be. Our children will know business and art, Japanese and English. We would never have met if it hadn't been for—"

"I know, I know. The piano."

Masa loved to credit the piano. It had fallen four stories from a crane and smashed onto the sidewalk with a sound like the end of the universe. Pedestrians on the street, Masa included, had been detoured along a narrow side street—the very street where Saki's puppets were displayed in a tiny gallery. Feeling the detour to be a sign, Masa had stepped inside the gallery.

"You have to admit—we would never have found each other otherwise." He liked the idea that he was fate's gift to someone, and that it had gone to such outrageous lengths to deliver him.

"People don't *find* each other. They just *happen* to each other."

"Well, maybe I wasn't looking for you, but I *was* looking—for something I didn't know . . . but . . . that could only have been you!" His voice rose, and the teenage couple at the next table glanced over at them.

"The piano was a coincidence. Otherwise you would have 'found' someone else."

"It doesn't feel very special, when you put it that way."

She set her bony elbows on the table. "Want to know the *real* reason we got together?"

"Certainly, my dear."

Her scarf dipped into her soup bowl as she whispered, "I grew a tail."

He laughed loudly, as if to let everyone in the restaurant know that things were just fine.

"It grew out of that mole on my lower back."

He dropped her hands and sat back, gripping his chair's stout leather armrests. "Amazing. Was it very long?"

Saki held up her hand and spread her thumb and pinkie apart.

"And tell me how that brought us together?"

"Well, when I grew it, I had to quit my job at the department store—the tail wouldn't fit under the tight skirt they made us wear—and that's when I took up puppetry."

"Makes perfect sense. You know, I've got a tail of my own, so to speak." He didn't mind being steered away from his originally planned conversation. Keeping up with Saki like this made him feel young.

"Also, I wasn't really a virgin."

"Mm?" He waited to get the joke.

"When we met. I wouldn't have sex with you because of the tail. I was embarrassed to let you see me naked. It was true that I was waiting for the right time . . . it's just that that time was dependent on losing the tail, not attaining a certain level of comfort with you."

"What're you talking about? Are you still kidding with me?" A swirling sensation that started in his chest spun and tightened and made its way to his eyes; it was like a typhoon in his head.

"You weren't a virgin?"

She lifted a spoonful of soup with her free hand, and slurped. "What'd you expect?"

"How many men have you been with, then?"

"Not too many," she said.

"Less than five?"

"Maybe. Yeah. Less than five."

"Less than three?" Maybe there had only been one other—a boyfriend in high school, someone so far gone she could hardly remember his name.

"I just told you I grew a *tail*, and you're more concerned about how many men I've screwed?"

Masa massaged his neck. He decided to finish the conversation so that he could proceed with his original topic—one of real importance.

But she kept laughing, covering her face and repeating, "I tell you I grew a tail, and you're more concerned . . ."

THAT NIGHT MASA DREAMED he was a bird with huge, heavy wings, flying over a sea that covered the world. His muscles burned; he'd been flying for days. But there was nowhere to stop. He scoured the horizon for a sign of land—nothing. Drops of rain bit at his eyes. He was falling. He tried to open his wings against gravity and his own gathering speed, but could not. Just as he realized he was going to die, he made another realization, which was that he had been flying in circles.

When he hit the water, he awoke. He sat up in his futon. A drop of real sweat slipped down the side of his nose. He looked over to ground himself in Saki's presence and found her futon empty.

He stood at the window. Though he'd eaten little, he had no appetite. He hadn't been able to further the discussion about children during dinner after all; Saki had decided she was full after the soup, and they had come back to their hotel.

There was no moon yet; the beach was a strip of blackness. Water lapped against piles of seaweed; after each wave came the sound of water trickling through the gnarled piles. At the far end of the beach, near the old shrine, he detected movement, a shape dark within the darkness. What if she was out there, in the middle of the night, hanging around that creepy old shrine? Her antics over dinner had soured more than just his stomach. For the first time, Masa allowed himself to consider that his mother may have been right.

For a moment it seemed the whole world was deserted, had taken off in ships from this very harbor while he was asleep. He put on his *yukata*.

The stooped innkeeper was wiping down the bar.

"Excuse me," Masa said. "The woman I was with—my wife—did you happen to see her just now?"

"Young Miss Saki? Yes, indeed. She was just down here using the restroom. I imagine she didn't want to disturb you while you were sleeping by using yours. Women do it more often than you'd think."

"Is that so?"

"The men? Never. They just flush away at two, three in the morning."

"Did you happen to notice where she went after that?"

"Sorry, I was in and out of the kitchen."

"I'll take a quick stroll, then, get some air. I can't seem to sleep," Masa said.

"Watch your step out there," said the innkeeper.

MASA FOUND HIS ADIDAS in the entryway and slipped them on unlaced. The action made him feel free and powerful, master of small risks. His mother's voice echoed in his head: "One of these days you'll fall flat on your face!" He took pleasure in the sound of his shoelaces tapping on the concrete. When the sidewalk dead-ended onto the sand, he removed his shoes and set them side by side, pointing toward the hotel.

The area around the shrine appeared deserted. Relieved, he walked to the shore. The sand was cold and soft and filled the gaps between his toes. He stopped in front of the mound of seaweed where Saki had noticed the gull earlier. The bird was gone. An animal must have carried it away, he thought. Then he heard a guttural call, shrill and severe like a crow's.

There she was, leaning out the window just the way he had minutes earlier. A tingling relief swept over him. Saki had never been out here at all; their paths must have crossed while she was in the bathroom. He blew a kiss. She mimed catching and eating it.

Chuckling, he knelt down and cupped his hands into the sand. Each grain is a day, he thought, watching the sand slip through his parting fingers. When it had gone, he brushed his hands on his thighs and looked out at the water. The moon hung low on the horizon. Persimmon moon, his mother would have said. Quick to ripen, quick to rot.

MASA SLID THE DOOR SHUT behind him and looked at Saki. Usually she slept flat on her back, her fingers curled over the blanket's edge like a child's, but tonight she was on her stomach. She was naked—Saki always slept naked—and Masa was struck by the beauty of her curves under the sheet. He whispered her name.

She shifted a little but did not respond. He remembered his nightmare and shuddered, and said a quick prayer that his wife would have nothing but pleasant dreams. Then he lifted the sheet from her back.

His eyes fell on the mole at the base of her spine. He tried to imagine a tail growing there, a soft, rainbow-hued appendage, full and bushy, like that of a cartoon character.

Marriage was about adjustment, and Saki was forcing him to lighten up—something he needed more than he'd realized. He slid into his futon and congratulated himself on following the crumbs of fate that had led him to his new wife, despite her rebelliousness and the opposition from his family.

Yet he couldn't sleep. Despite the relief he'd felt on the beach, something still gnawed at him in that dark room. Her behavior tonight had made him doubt her, and he didn't like doubt. Now when he looked at Saki, he saw two women: one good, the woman he'd married, the other manipulative and wicked.

It's only the late hour, he thought. He pulled the sheet

back over Saki, pausing to peer at the mole. Just for a second, he thought he saw it twitch.

"CAN'T SLEEP MUCH THESE DAYS MYSELF," the innkeeper said. "Older you get, the longer the nights."

"Sure seems that way."

The innkeeper poured sake from a plain brown bottle and set two cups on the wooden bar. "You two married long?"

"This is our honeymoon."

The man slapped the bar so hard their cups rattled. "In this dump? No offense intended. We drink together at this hour, we speak as friends."

"My wife likes places like this. Out of the way, old, 'with character,' she says."

"Plenty of that around."

They drank. Masa finished his cup first. "Was the typhoon bad in this area?"

"Not as bad as other parts of the island. These big storms tend to miss us. Something with the currents."

"That's lucky."

"Mm. I'll tell you, though, we sure get the wreckage. You saw the beach."

"A real mess," Masa said, remembering the gull.

"That big typhoon last year? Hardly rained a drop here. Then two days later a car washes up on the beach."

"No kidding!"

"Yup. Legendary. You see that carved stone up near the cliff?"

"We noticed it. Old lettering." He added, "My wife could read it better than I could, and she's only half Japanese."

"That so?"

"Yeah. She's bilingual, but she likes studying the old stuff."

"Really? That's odd."

"What do you mean, odd?"

Instead of answering, the innkeeper filled their cups again. He seemed to focus very hard on pouring the liquid. Must be drunk already, Masa thought. He was feeling a little drunk himself.

"So what *is* the story with that stone? Part of some old shrine?"

The innkeeper raised his cup but made no toast. "They say it's haunted by a demon."

At the word *demon*, Masa shivered.

"There was a typhoon a few generations back. Story goes a woman washed ashore—a foreigner, who couldn't communicate with anyone in the village.

"She was beautiful in a strange way, with eyes the color of the sea, and she could do things—heal sick children, weave kimonos that were warm as down yet light as a feather. People worshipped her. They built that shrine in the spot she washed up.

"But after a while folks began to distrust her. A child in the village died under her care. The townspeople began calling her the Blue Demon, because of her eyes, and arranged for her execution."

Masa's mouth was dry; he lifted his cup and found it

empty. He grabbed the bottle and tipped it to his glass. After a few seconds he realized that it, too, was empty. "So they killed her?" he asked.

"She got away. There was an old man in town, a hermit, who could understand her language. On the night of her planned execution, the two of them jumped into a boat and drifted away without oars. A storm came up that night, and they were never seen again."

"Any truth to it?"

"One man's truth is another's illusion—isn't that how the saying goes?"

Masa felt chilled, as if a fog had blown in silently off the water and made its way into the bar. It was all getting to be too much: Saki's offhand "confession" about the men before him was confusing, and the ridiculous—simply ridiculous—idea of her growing a tail had derailed his plan to discuss children. She always seemed to be a step ahead of him.

Then she was there, her voice sliding into the room like a snake, coiling up his leg toward his chest and clutching him there.

"Troubled always is the late-hour child," she called, reciting a proverb.

The innkeeper pulled out another bottle, white wine, and set a third glass on the bar. "A miserable cat loves the company of mice," he replied.

Saki sidled up next to Masa. She touched his arm, and with her grassy scent, the warmth returned to him. He did not look her in the eye. Her presence made him feel drunker.

"Lonely," Saki corrected. "A lonely cat keeps company with mice."

"That's right," the innkeeper said. They sat in silence and watched a drop of condensation slip down the side of the bottle and into a crevice in the wood.

The old man stood. "Pardon the rudeness, but my eyelids might be filled with sand." He held out the wine to Masa. "A wedding gift. Likely to be a storm coming in tomorrow, and you two will need to pass the time somehow."

Masa accepted the bottle with two hands as he rose from his stool. "A storm? But the papers called for—"

"Come, Masahiro," Saki called, already up and walking away. Masa watched her tangled hair shimmy across her back. When he turned back to the bar, their host had departed, the door behind the bar swinging lightly with his exit.

REUNION
\\\\\\\\\\\\

OVER THE COURSE OF THAT interminable weekend after Jun died, Asian lady beetles overtook our place in
shadowy Totsuka-cho. Orange, winged bodies coated the
ceiling and left yellow stains; carapaces crunched underfoot against the bathroom tile. The air smelled like ran-
cid walnuts.

Ms. Morita, my next-door neighbor, offered to rent
me her basement apartment, cheap. The place was bug-
free: "sealed like a carton of fresh tofu," she told me. She
hadn't even seen a cockroach in nine years. I said I'd take
a look. My mind operated beneath a fog; I was dazed, in
shock. Ms. Morita thought it was the beetles.

The apartment was loaded with knickknacks from travels with her husband, who had died suddenly the year before, and whose life's work had been vacuum-cleaner design. "If you've ever used a Kanko Uzu-Jet," Ms. Morita told me, "you've used Kazu's tubes." I felt close to her after hearing that. I signed a lease on the spot.

The main room housed vacuum cleaners in various states of disrepair. "Kazu used this room as a sort of lab," she said as she showed me in. We kneeled on frayed tatami. "I haven't had the heart to clean it out yet."

I said I didn't mind, but really, it creeped me out, these machines sitting around, waiting. One stood in the corner, the size of a big kid, with a puffed bag in place of a torso, a rectangular foot-group, and corrugated tubing lolling out of places limbs shouldn't be. But Ms. Morita was very nice. She made tea and listened. I described for her the loneliness of mourning someone else's husband. Six days prior to the beetles' arrival, he'd promised a divorce. He even presented me with a jar, its lid stabbed full of holes, as a promise that we'd be together—openly—in time for the firefly festival. Our friends would see us there and know, he said. He was sad about the breakup of his marriage, but it had happened over a period of years and there was little left to grieve. He would be proud to be seen with me.

After Ms. Morita slippered out of the room, I looked around. Bristles, hoses, and gears surrounded me. Plastic panels of irregular shape lay scattered, like pieces of a shattered continent, the last arrangement of something lost.

I thought of our first night together: Tanabata, the festival of lovers banished to the heavens and forever separated by the Milky Way. Before kissing on the pebbled shore, we'd stopped for the man running the shell game: *To track the ball just use your eyes; find it now and claim your prize.* I quit early on, but Jun wouldn't give up. After four tries we finally walked away, and he lamented in that dialect, the syllables like rain in a puddle, "I just can't believe I lost."

I picked up the end of a long red tube connected to the kid-sized vacuum, moved it up and down. *Hajimemashite.* Pleased to meet you, sir. I leaned against its bag-body, which crinkled in greeting, and closed my eyes. The lights of paper lanterns shimmered red-yellow in the summer night heat, smelling of fried squid and bean cakes, and a barker called out, his voice like a hook:

One night only, for sale at cost, everything you've ever lost!

On the first table stood a stuffed horse I'd won in a coloring contest, long before I heard the word *expatriate*, long before I knew the Japanese slang for *foreigner* was *outsider*. I'd named the horse after its color: Gravel. Days later, Gravel fell from the back of my mother's bike. No more than three years old, I'd made her retrace the route at least ten times. How could something just disappear?

The pony's price tag said, "¥350, OBO." I plunked a bill on the table and looked around. No one was there to make change, and that was fine by me. I scooped up Gravel and brought him to my face. His mushy little body smelled of salt and oil. The blue-gray fur on his back was matted where he must have landed on the winter road. I pressed him to my cheek.

I picked up object after object: pens of blue, black, red, one of lavender, tops chewed. Hair ties, single socks. A pile of teeth like corn kernels. I dropped coins as I moved, a small one for the 110-speed camera I'd dropped from a roller coaster, a larger one for the gold locket, big enough to derail a train, a gift from my high school boyfriend. My arms and pockets were loaded, my waistband holding in a few of the bigger items, the Nintendo console I'd thought stolen, a pink leather boot whose mate still sat in my closet in the infested apartment. I would leave it there to serve as a beetle dwelling, or grave. That boot was the first thing from him I'd lost.

The last table held just one thing, a fist-sized, crimson lump that shivered and thrashed like a fish out of water. I stared until it became a red blur. No price tag. My wallet was empty anyway. I turned away, my arms full and an empty feeling in my chest, a feeling like three shells and a realization—no ball, there never was a ball—and listened for a voice, any voice, to bring me back.

ROOEY
\\\\\\\\\

SINCE ROOEY DIED, I'M NO LONGER MYSELF. Foods I've hated my entire life, I crave. Different things are funny. I've stopped wearing a bra. I bet they're thinking about firing me here at work, but they must feel bad, my brother so recently dead and all. Plus, I'm cheap labor, fresh out of college. And let's face it, the *Sweetwater Weekly* doesn't have the most demanding readership or publishing standards.

You can tell they're trying to be sensitive: along with the police blotter and wedding announcements, I'd covered obituaries; afterward they gave the obituaries to Ryan the intern so I wouldn't have to think about death all day. I do anyway. Bloody, violent death, wakes and funerals and the way a person's eyes look right before they die, how when you try to close them they don't stay closed like in the movies—they pop back open.

I've started adding things to the blotter, things that never happened but that he'd find funny, and the chimp wedding announcement I slipped in—photo included—didn't get caught until right before press.

A few days ago I tried logging into Rooey's email and got the password on the first guess. (It was "Miyazaki," his favorite animator. Rooey was obsessed with Japan. When we tagged our suitcases for Hawaii, he'd spelled his name "Rui." He'd even figured how to write his name in Japanese using the characters for "drifting" and "majesty.") Now I check his email all the time. I've just logged in when Myra, the assistant editor, comes by my cubicle. She's wearing the same man's button-down shirt as always.

"Hi, hon." Even when she smiles she keeps her lips pressed tightly together. I've never seen her teeth.

"Hi."

She opens her mouth and closes it like she's changed her mind about something. "Maxine, how are you *doing*?"

"Oh, you know. It's good to keep busy with real challenging tasks at work, like typing up wedding announcements."

She sighs and looks at me pityingly. "I wanted to talk to you about that."

I stare at the screen.

She lowers her voice. "I got your point with the monkey thing, OK? I thought it would be best to lighten your workload, but obviously that's not working. So, Maxine, how about a cover story?"

"Great." I empty Rooey's spam folder. The screen looks clean and expectant.

"Really?"

"Sure." My phone chimes, announcing the arrival of a text message.

She nods harder than necessary and says, "Well, great then! Why don't you think it over this week and we can chat about it on Friday? I'm sure you're full of ideas. Sound good?"

"Sounds great, thank you," I say, because that's what the old Maxine would've said. But now I guess I've just lost interest.

Here's a story: two people are in trouble and the wrong one dies. There's been a cosmic mix-up, but there's nothing anyone can do about it, and they all live sadly ever after. The end.

I snap open my phone and read Felix's message. It says: "Uijoljoh pg zpv."

He's used this code before. The trick is that each letter is really the one before it. It says, "Thinking of you."

I write back "V 3" for "U 2," close the phone, and go back to my email.

I WALK TO FELIX'S AFTER WORK. He rents a garden apartment, which means he lives half-underground and there's not much light, but it's cheap. When we save enough, we're supposed to get a place together, somewhere up high.

Back before Rooey started high school, our family lived near here, across from the tracks on Burlington in a house with an aboveground pool and a pop-up camper that never moved from the backyard. Mom said she and Dad had used it all the time and that I'd taken a few trips in it too, but I don't remember them, and by the time Rooey came along, Dad was gone and I didn't remember him, either.

There was a small door we could use to squeeze into the camper even when it wasn't popped up, and we'd take turns locking one another inside. The object was to see how long we could stay in before getting scared and knocking to come out. We called the game Coffin. It was pitch-black inside the camper, and the air was stuffy and smelled of hot wool.

I was five years older and generally humane, but once—I think I was mad because Mom had let Rooey get away with something, again—I didn't let him out when he gave the triple-knock. He tried again. There was a moment of silence that I took to be him getting pissed, and I laughed.

Then he started pounding and, after a few seconds, screaming. I fumbled with the lock while the door shuddered. *"LEEEET MEEEE OOUUUUT!"*

"Hang *on*!"

When the door finally swung open, my little brother fell out onto his side, his face white save for two spots of color on his cheeks. He stared at me in disbelief, his brown eyes watery.

When he stood and came at me, I didn't fight back. I let him flail his fists and scream himself hoarse. Eventually we played something else. He didn't tell Mom—he never did. That was the last time we played Coffin.

There are six stairs leading down to Felix's door. When I get to the bottom, I'm always aware of how much of me is below ground. It's like a very wide grave, this apartment. Recently I've had to fight the urge to turn around and go back up.

Felix is cooking with his back to the door and doesn't hear me come in. He's got his khakis on from work and no shirt. He has what he calls a "techie tan," which means he is white like recycled paper. He works at an Internet dating company, fixing the employees' computers. He finds it exciting. He finds almost anything exciting. It's probably why I like him.

I watch his papery back at the stove and think, he is biodegradable. Then I think that his body mirrors the apartment, the bottom buried and the top exposed to light.

He turns and sees me and sings, "Ma-a-a-axine! You don't have to put on the red light!" He takes my face in his hands and kisses me loudly.

We have pesto for dinner, and he talks about how he managed to solve three people's problems without even showing up at their cubicles.

"If people would just *troubleshoot*, it would save so much time. A simple logical process, that's all it takes!"

Since Rooey died, Felix has become even more enthusiastic, maybe to make up for my silences.

I tell him about the cover story. He wants to celebrate

so we get in bed and drink a bottle of champagne under the covers.

"I'm feeling better."

"Yeah?"

"About Rooey."

"Good!"

"I think I'm getting over it. I think I'm done crying."

"Wow! Well. You know. Take your time. There's no time limit." He looks at me solemnly and I notice his pores. When did they get so big? On his nightstand, turned upside down, is a book: *When a Loved One Grieves.*

"Have you thought any more about trying therapy?" he asks.

"Mm. Not my thing."

"I know you believe that, but how can you know if you don't try?"

"I'd rather not talk about this stuff right now." I slip my hand in his boxers. I could care less about sex with Felix lately and now is no different, but at least it will shut him up.

I wonder how he'll react if I tell him to fuck me, so I whisper it—"I want you to fuck me"—and he blushes; we've never used this word before, and I realize he doesn't necessarily know how it differs from what we usually do, what he always refers to as "making love." But he gives it a shot. He gets on top of me, sticks it in, and buries his face in my neck, biting me, I think, though I can't be sure.

"Harder," I tell him, squirming a bit, and he tries to pin my arms over my head while holding himself up with one hand, but he loses balance and folds down on top of me.

His face finds my armpit for a second and his nose wrinkles up.

I sniff under my arm. "Whew. Kind of manly, I know."

"No big deal."

"I've been using Rooey's deodorant."

"Oh." He pauses, traces my belly button with his middle finger. "Why?"

"Works better. And it doesn't smell like flowers."

"What's wrong with flowers?"

I shrug. "They're so *girly*."

We fall asleep. I dream I'm alone, bobbing in a black sea. I don't know which way to swim, and the bottom's miles below. A fin appears in the distance. I swim away from it, but it catches up, and as it gets closer I see it's Rooey, and I see in his eyes that he hates me. I watch helplessly as he speeds closer, teeth and gums bared, and when he finally reaches me, there's a flare of heat in my neck, and afterward a sensation like dissolving. Only when I give in, do I wake up. That giving in is a release so powerful I find myself sitting up in bed, heaving. That giving in is the saddest feeling in the world.

IT'S BEEN THREE MONTHS AND THREE DAYS. Mom hasn't touched up her strawberry blonde dye job since the attack, and the dark roots are like a measuring stick: her grief is lengthening. She sleeps all morning and spends her afternoons shopping and preparing elaborate dinners. She cooks things Rooey liked—curry pork, eggplant Parmesan. I've come to find comfort in this, and for once in my life, I eat everything on my plate. Mom is the opposite. Once, after filling our plates with salmon ragout, she sat down and stared at the table's empty seats, two of them now, as if she were expecting guests who were running late. I had no words to offer up; I shoveled down the over-salted food and sat there as long as I could stand it, then stood and cleared her untouched plate.

While Rooey looked just like Dad, I resemble no one. My face is a little of this, little of that, like a meal thrown together last-minute. When we ran into old friends of my parents', they would make a fuss over Rooey. "A carbon copy of Dean," Mom would say, mussing my brother's blonde, moppy curls. Then they'd turn to me and joke about the milkman.

School was my redemption. In high school I was a member of the National Honor Society, vice-president of the Ecology Club, and a varsity swimmer. When Rooey and Mom came to my swim meets, they'd always sit in the same place, at the top of the bleachers, laughing and eating Reese's Pieces. Tearing through the water on the final leg of a race, I would think of them watching me and swim harder, muscles screaming, knowing that if I won, I would for a moment be the focus; I would fill that tiny space between them.

At the wake, I talked about taking Rooey for driving practice last Christmas. For a kid who liked cars so much, he was a horrible driver. He made a joke out of it. Before leaving the house, he'd preface everything with, "Allah willing." It was an expression he picked up from a movie. "When we come back from driving, Allah willing, let's get Mom to take us to Culver's." "Allah willing, I'm gonna parallel-park this baby, *hard*." It was a testament to Rooey's good nature that he was able to mock himself, I said; even more than that, though, he never seemed to get discouraged. He had confidence in life; he never whined. The part about "Allah willing" got a laugh.

What I didn't talk about was how mad I'd been when Mom told me I'd have to give Rooey my car when I moved out. The Nissan had been a hand-me-down from my grandparents, and I'd had it less than a year. I never had a car when I was his age, I argued. It wasn't *fair*.

But Rooey solved the problem—he didn't want my car. He wanted an old Thunderbird, and he got a job helping Roger, a Buddhist hippie guy who lived down the block, in his metalwork shop to earn the money for it. He was a hard kid to resent, and for that, I have to admit, I resented him even more.

ROOEY'S DOOR HAS BEEN CLOSED since I got back from Hawaii. Mom's not ready to open it yet. "It's too much of him at once," she told me, crying at the mere mention of his name. But me, I can't get enough. I've been coming in here every night. I lie in bed and wait until the sleeping pills I stole from Mom kick in, then creep over the cracked parquet to his room, my feet instinctively avoiding the creaky spots that, when we were little, would give us away as we snuck into the kitchen for a handful of Reese's Pieces from the green jar.

The room is stuffy and smells vaguely of peanut butter.

When he was in grade school, Rooey insisted on painting his walls to look like outer space; I painted Jupiter and Neptune, and Rooey did the rest, except Earth, which Mom did, and after the paint dried Rooey etched our tiny trio in ballpoint pen where he approximated Indiana to be. There's a tiny chip of paint missing where my head once was.

I flop down onto his bed and try to imagine what it was like to be him.

Rooey had something of a girlfriend, though we never called her that; she was just "his friend." Lily. Her parents came here from Japan right before she was born, and gave her a name neither of them could pronounce. Once I walked in on Rooey and her together, in bed. Or rather *on* the bed—they lay belly-up beside one another, Lily's arms at her sides, the hand nearest Rooey touching both her leg and his. Rooey's hands were folded atop his stomach. They both stared at the ceiling.

She was a strange-looking girl, with a tiny pucker of a mouth and hair to her waist. Her eyes and nose were just little pinches too, and you wondered how her head didn't tip back under the weight of all that hair. She had braces—maybe that helped balance things out. At the funeral she cried and covered not her eyes but her mouth.

The entire night passes this way, me, flat on his bed as if afloat, my mind full of details, all the questions I never thought to ask him: what was happening with Lily, and whether he had a clue what he was doing; how his job was going at the metalworking shop; was he any good at the work?

The stucco swirls above me, lit by the half moon outside. Then that spot of ceiling, that personal place where the eyes rest when you're thinking in the dark, whispers answers:

Things with Lily were slow moving, excruciating, thrilling; they'd French-kissed once after school and it tasted salty; if he were still alive, he'd take her to see a movie when he got his T-bird. When things got serious, he'd make her something in the metal shop, a figurine of some kind, and give it to her for her birthday. He was good at transferring the molds and pouring and measuring and scraping, all the intricate business of making casts. He had the patience for it.

When the first gray light struggles into the room, I open my eyes, or maybe it just feels like I'm opening them, since I haven't really slept. I wouldn't call what I do in this room at night "sleep." It's more like a nocturnal hypnosis that only clears when the sun comes snapping its fingers.

I stand up and go to the closet. CD album covers shingle the door and partially obscure the mirror attached to it. At eye level is the cover for the Vapors's "Turning Japanese" single I gave Rooey for Christmas last year.

I pull the door open, and cool, sour-smelling air drifts out. Rooey's favorite T-shirt hangs crooked on a wooden hanger. The shirt is gray and is noticeably shorter than the other shirts in the closet. The turquoise lettering on the front says POCARI SWEAT. He came home from school late one day, having stopped and bought it at Teed Off, the T-shirt place downtown. He said he'd looked online—he was always looking up something online—and read that Pocari Sweat was like Japanese Gatorade, and when he called Lily and told her about it, she'd laughed and laughed; Rooey held the phone away from his ear, and I could hear her from across the room.

I yank the shirt from its hanger and put it on. Then I lie on the bed and slide two fingers under the waist of my panties.

I don't fantasize anymore when I masturbate. It's just a lot of furious rubbing, no imagination required, though sometimes toward the end an image of Lily, sunbathing naked, pops into my mind. Before Rooey died, my orgasms had come in sweet, rolling waves. Now they're like squalls, the pleasure almost violent.

Afterward I think about my cover story. There was a time, I realize, when I dreamed about this opportunity— my name on the front page, a color photo illustrating my words—but the ideas I used to toss around aren't appealing anymore. Profile piece on the owner of Ambrosia, the green grocer? A report on the solar-powered nunnery out in Teastown? When did I ever find *that* interesting? It'd be cool to write something on the guy in town with the Porsche Carrera GT. A half-million dollar car in this town—now *that's* news.

I close my eyes and imagine I'm driving an incredibly fast car on a circular track, around and around, on the brink of losing control.

THE TRIP TO HAWAII WAS a graduation gift from my grandma. I took classes these past two summers in order to graduate early and hadn't left the Midwest since I could remember. I chose to bring Rooey over Felix because, as I saw it, Rooey and I were at the end of our shared childhood. Soon I'd be moving out for good, leaving him for the real world. I wanted to hang on to that life just a little longer.

They tell me I did the right thing, swimming ashore and yelling for help, but I don't remember this. I remember sounds: a scream, a moan, then the sloshing of water like kids in a bathtub; I could hear children calling to one another on the sand, a game of Red Rover, while Rooey's head went under and his forearm drifted away from blonde hair that clung to the surface; the fingers that had reached up from the bottom bunk brushed my abdomen while I watched ragged strips of tissue jet blood. I remember turning and swimming away. That I headed for the shore was purely coincidence.

I MUST HAVE DOZED OFF, because when I open my eyes a few hours have passed and I'm thinking of Lily. Her long dark hair, and the way she locks eyes with you when she laughs. My chest aches, and I realize: I miss her.

It's a weird feeling, missing someone I barely know, yet when I think about it, it seems odd that I'd feel any other way. Why don't I go for a visit? I look around the room for something to bring her. I look down and—that's it—I'll give her shirt—the shirt she found so funny!

I walk there, swinging the CVS bag that holds the T-shirt. I'm walking quickly, looking up at the clouds as I go, wondering what Lily will have to say, and whether she'll be glad to see me. A car horn blasts. I jump back and a woman in a Jeep waves me across the street I'd been about to step into. I hustle across, blushing. I'm glad to have an excuse to rush, and I jog the last block to Lily's house.

Mrs. Mizukami answers the door. She's wearing bright orange slippers. Her mouth drops at the sight of me, and she keeps a hand on the doorknob as I remind her who I am, though of course we've met before. I hold up the bag, full of nervous energy. She ushers me into a dim living room full of ferns and looks at me with sad eyes. I want to say, don't be sad! Things are going to be fine, really!

Mrs. Mizukami leads me into the kitchen, where Lily is seated at the table, doing homework.

She scoots her chair back when she sees me and stands up. I can tell she's surprised, and I say so.

"Yeah!" she says, taking me in. "But, you know, in a good way." She doesn't say anything else.

Mrs. Mizukami sets a glass of iced tea and a plate of cookies on the table. "Please, sit," she says, and we do. She shuffles out the room.

"I'm sorry I interrupted your homework," I say. "I should have called."

"Nah, it's OK." Lily pushes an open textbook away and leans both elbows on the table. "Math sucks anyway."

I ask her about school. I watch her mouth move as she answers, then follow the smooth line of her hair down, over her small breasts, to where it puddles in her lap, like a waterfall. I want to touch it.

"Are you OK?" She leans back.

"Yeah, sorry." I blush, and fish for something an older sister would say. "Your hair's great. I wish I could grow mine that long."

She makes a face and bats her hair back, then picks up a pair of red-handled scissors from the table. "I think I'm gonna chop it."

"What? No! It—it's so pretty."

"Whatever. It's been long my whole life." She gathers a fistful. "Time for something new."

She slides the scissors open, brings the blades to her hair. "Very funny," I say.

She's watching me, eyes wide, and then snaps the scissors shut. I lurch out of my chair to stop her, but she moves the blades at the last second.

"I made you pretty nervous," she says, grinning.

"You had me for a second. Well, maybe a half-second."

"Well, I still might do it." She pulls a few strands forward and really does snip them off. We watch them float to the ground. She says, "It could be like . . . an offering."

"But—wouldn't he want you to keep it?"

She shrugs. "He's not here to ask."

I look at the hair on the floor and am seized by a desire to pinch it up and hold onto it forever. Then I remember the shirt. I grab for the bag and dump out the T-shirt in front of her. "So, I brought this for you. I thought you might like to have it."

She stares at the balled-up fabric and bites her lip. She blinks back tears, and I lean over and hug her tight. I close my eyes. We rock together, her head on my shoulder and my face in her hair. It feels wonderful. I move my hand on her back, hold her tighter.

"Can I—" Mrs. Mizukami stops in the doorway. Lily and I spring apart like two kids caught necking.

"Beg your pardon," Mrs. Mizukami says, bowing slightly and backing out of the room. "I just wondered if I could give you more food."

"No, Mom," Lily says.

"No thank you," I say as she leaves, and though I haven't touched them, I call, "The cookies are delicious, though."

Lily and I look at each other. She looks at her lap.

"I should get going," I say.

"Thank you," she says, standing up, grasping the shirt with one fist.

At the front door, I put my shoes on and say goodbye to Mrs. Mizukami. Lily steps outside with me.

"It's nice to see you," she says. "Just, you know, a surprise. Sorry I'm all crying and stuff. I mean, he was *your* brother."

"It's good to see you too. Someone he was close to, who he really liked. He was *very* picky about people, you know." We laugh; she sniffles and catches my eye.

"I dunno, this is weird, but when you walked in, I thought it was him. I could've sworn it. Isn't that messed up?"

"I think I see him all the time."

She touches her hair. "I just . . . miss him."

I think of them lying on the narrow bed together, touching without acknowledging it, and think of me lying there with her instead, what that might feel like. I want to tell her this, but what would I say?

She's looking at me again, really focusing, like she's looking for something she dropped. She takes a deep breath and hands me the shirt.

"You should really keep this."

I say no and reach for it anyway.

"Really, I'm definitely sure." Her eyes are watering, her tiny nose pink, as she backs into the door. It's shut, and she fumbles for the handle while keeping her eyes on me.

"Thanks again." She turns the handle and takes a step backward, into the shadows. "I'll see you around."

"Yeah," I say, and force a grin, a wave with the shirt. "Allah willing!"

I walk home slowly. It's only September, but the sidewalk's already full of leaves that crunch underfoot. It seems like the leaves are always falling. I don't know how the trees keep up.

IT'S FRIDAY. MY MEETING WITH MYRA is not going well.

"I'm not saying the story on Metalfest is a bad idea," she's saying. "At all. Just not right for our *readership*."

I can tell she's not wearing a bra under her light blue blouse. I wonder what her nipples look like.

"How about the comic book convention?"

"Well, I mean, it *could* work, my only concern is that, well, it raises the same issue as the music festival. Japanese comic books are certainly popular these days, but for most of our subscribers . . ." She licks her lips, slowly. Her tongue is plump and pink and her lips shine.

"You know," she continues when I don't respond, "didn't you mention something once about a profile of that lady who owns Ambrosia?"

Something is happening inside me, a wild building energy like a wave.

The AP report read like a Mad Libs:

"Died of blood loss." Nope: Cardiac arrest.

"Swimming alone." Wrong: It could've been me.

"The victim was 16 years old." Wrong again: he was fifteen. If he'd been sixteen, he probably would've stayed home, peeling around corners with his friends in his Thunderbird. He'd be a different person. He'd be alive.

"Oh, fuck it," I say. "Fuck journalism."

Myra jerks back in her chair.

"I don't give a shit," I say. I get up and walk away, all the way to the door, and out into the blinding afternoon sunlight.

ON THE DRIVE HOME I get a text from Felix. "rinned ta iva lebla?" it says. I've been avoiding Felix since our awkward night in bed and whatever the message means— probably an invitation of some sort—I'm not in the mood to figure it out. "Call u later," I respond.

When I get home, Mom's not there. I go to Rooey's room, the only place that really feels like my own anymore.

The shelves are lined with Japanese comics and language learning manuals. I slide one of the thin books from the shelf. In the cover illustration a blue-haired, starry-eyed girl holding a red ball reaches out to a boy swathed in tentacles. The boy's teeth are clenched; his face fierce. The girl is saying, "Swallow this orb to reverse the spell!" The title is *101 Japanese Phrases You'll Never Use*.

My phone rings: Myra. I don't pick up, and she leaves a voicemail suggesting that I take a week off, "to think things over." She wants me to know that I am in everyone's prayers. As soon as I'm done listening to her message, Felix beeps in, and I answer without thinking.

"Hey," he says. "You didn't call."

"Oh, yeah. Sorry. I got sidetracked."

He's silent for a second, then says, "Did you figure out my text?"

"Oh. No, I forgot."

"I was suggesting dinner at Via Bella. We haven't been there since our anniversary. I'm going through withdrawal." He laughs.

"Ah."

"It was an anagram," he adds.

I pick up Rooey's guitar, a red electric with frets worn down past the grain.

"Can I call you back in a few minutes?"

"Sure, babe."

I hang up and cradle the guitar. Despite all my accomplishments in school, music has always eluded me. Band's the only activity I've ever quit.

But Rooey's guitar feels right. Its slim weight against my chest is a comfort, and the curved wood nestles into my thigh. The neck is thin and the strings soft. I know no chords but find it soothing to close my eyes and let my hands wander, the smooth wood grain cradling my fingertips, and occasionally I hit upon a combination of strings that sounds like a choir.

When it gets too late to have dinner, Felix texts me, Are you OK? I pick up *101 Japanese Phrases You'll Never Use*, open it to a random page, and respond back with the first sentence I see: *Ebi wa dashi no nakade yuukan ni tatakaimasu!*

It means: How valiantly the shrimp struggle in the broth!

THEY HELD MASS AT my grandparents' church. While the deacon said things like, "The Lord takes first whom he loves best" and "To die young is a blessing," images of that day slideshowed through my mind—Rooey's head, just above water, snapping back on his neck, Rooey's eyes wide and black as he looked at me that last time, while I treaded water a few feet away. I wondered if he knew he was dying, that when he closed his eyes on the pain, they would never reopen. I thought of this as the deacon droned, as my mother's pale jaw clenched and unclenched, her eyes like ice—she had not cried yet—and I stood up in the pew and whispered, "Bullshit."

My voice carried through the church. I began to sob, and the sound echoed off the rafters and the stained glass window where Jesus hung on the cross with a trickle of blood on his palm and a serene smile on his face.

Him, not me, though I was just ten feet away. Him, not

me, though it had been my idea to swim out that far in a race we both knew I'd win. Not me, though I'd been on my period that day. It doesn't take much blood to draw a shark.

I stood there, shaking, everything in slow motion, while the deacon wrapped up the homily in his calm, gravelly voice, and I only began to move when he descended from the podium. He never looked in our direction. When I sat down, my mother shed her first tear.

I'M STILL PLAYING THE GUITAR when there's a knock on the front door. I go to answer it: Felix. He looks worried.

"Hey," he says. "What's going on?"

I shrug.

"Can I come in?"

I let him in and lead him into Rooey's room. We sit on the bed, and he looks around. His gaze stops on me. I don't meet his eyes. It's not a comfortable silence, but it's not uncomfortable, either.

"I've never been in here before."

"I like it here."

"I realized that message was in Japanese, romanized, so I translated it, but I don't know if I got the words all right because sometimes there are a few different meanings for the same word."

"Good job," I say, and pick up the guitar. I strum indiscriminately, and he starts rubbing my back. Then he gives me a series of small pats, like I'm a baby he's burping.

Finally I say, "I saw Lily today."

"Oh yeah? Where at?"

"Her house."

"You went over there? That was nice. How is she?"

Cute, I want to say. Crazy cute and wonderful. Instead I say, "I can see the attraction."

"That's good, I guess. Did you talk much about Rooey?"

"A little."

"She misses him too. It's good to talk about it."

He takes my hand, kisses it. Then I'm crying, sobbing into my palms. "She's going to cut off all her hair." I sniffle.

"Who is?"

"Lil-Lily."

"I see." He hugs me tighter. "Let it all out."

"I don't want to move in together."

We sit in silence after that. After a while I notice he's crying too.

"It's not your fault," I say.

"No, no. You're confused right now," he said. "This *is* my fault. I shouldn't have tried to be so cheery. I'm going to find some help for you. A therapist, or a group or something."

"I feel sick," I say, and I do.

"Do you want something to drink?"

"I think I'll just lie down. I'll give you a call later on."

"You want me to go?"

I nod. "I'll call you."

"If it's what you really want. Is it?"

I nod, yes, yes. He's barely out the door when I start

to gag. I run to the bathroom, where I empty my stomach of water and some half-chewed bread. It feels good to do that, to cleanse myself of the unnecessary. Afterward I call Lily, but there's no answer. I leave a message: Thanks for today. If you ever need to talk, or want company, please give me a call. I really hope you will.

THE COTTON OF THIS SHIRT is worn so thin it's silky. I catch a glimpse of myself in the mirror. Lily was right. I do resemble him.

My hair has gotten lighter. From being out in the sun, Felix says. It's also developed a wave for the first time in my life.

I remember something Felix told me, something out of his book: "Grieving and healing go hand-in-hand. Cut yourself a wide swath. Things *will* get better."

"Fuck that," I say to the mirror. "I don't give a flying fuck if I get *better*." I like that, "a flying fuck." Rooey used to say that.

"*Fuck* getting better. The sooner I get better, the sooner someone else is going to die."

It could've been me, and maybe it should've. After all, it was my scent in the water. It was my idea to race. It was my graduation trip.

Could've been me, should've been me. Hell—maybe it *was* me. I look in the mirror. Are my eyes getting darker? I lean in close to the mirror. Brown speckles the blue.

I sink to the floor. The boards creak.

True: I have not had my period since the attack.

True: I haven't slept in days.

True: I no longer desire anything. Well, no, that's not exactly true. I am horny as hell.

From the floor I can see under the bed. There are so few things under there, I can count them. Seven—eight, if you count each hockey skate. Two shoeboxes, a sock, an orange peel, a measuring tape, an unopened bottle of Corona.

I reach my foot under the bed and nudge the big shoebox toward me, the one that originally housed the hockey skates. It's heavy. Stuff clinks around inside. Tools, maybe.

I lift the lid, feeling ceremonious.

The box is filled to the brim with figurines. The ones Roger makes in the metal shop, little Buddhist statues about an inch tall—what are they called again?

(*Jizo*)

Juzu? Something like that?

(*Jizo*)

I close my eyes and the explanation comes: *They're called jizo. Like a combination of Jesus and Bozo.*

Jizo.

I pick one up and examine its face. Two crescents arch across the smooth metal face to form eyes. The ears are overlong; the earlobe grows out of the jaw.

I think they have something to do with Buddhism, but beyond that, I have no idea. I set the figurine down and fetch my laptop.

The online encyclopedia tells me that translated from Japanese, *jizo* means "earth treasury" or "earth womb."

"Traditionally," says the article, "jizo are seen as the guardians of travelers, firefighters, and children."

Children. I should bring one to Lily. Lily would like one.

I read on: "In particular, jizo are said to tend to the souls of miscarried or aborted fetuses, or any child who precedes his parents in death. It is said that children who die in this manner are not allowed to cross the sacred river to heaven as penance for the pain they have caused their parents."

If I focus all my willpower, I can bring him back, I think, staring at the jizo's sleepy face. I just have to want it enough.

I focus on the statue's face so long it begins to move. It wriggles in my palm and the lips move to speak, but before I hear the words, Mom's voice cuts in. She is standing in the doorway. What she says is, "Hi, sweetie."

"Look," I whisper, holding out the statue. "Did you know? He's the guardian of children."

Without a word she crosses the room, wraps her arms around me from behind, and begins sobbing into my hair. In the mirror I watch as she clutches at my hair, pulling and twisting, and each time she releases a handful, it is blonder and wavier than before.

I close my eyes. I'm kicking through clear, warm waves, my throat and nose stinging from salt water. I'm already a few lengths behind her. Then I feel a sudden, massive presence beneath me, its skin like sandpaper as it shoots past my leg. Dark stripes. The pain in my shoulder like a star exploding. I open my eyes, and my vision is blurry, like that of a newborn. For a second I smell the hot wool of the old camper.

"Oh, Rooey," she says. "What are we going to do without her?"

I hug her back without turning away from the mirror. I gaze at our reflection, her arms around the figure in the gray T-shirt.

"It's OK," I whisper. "I'm not going anywhere. I'm going to stay right here."

PIONEERS
\\\\\\\\\\

YUMIKO JIGGLED THE HANDLE and thought, *break, broke, broken.*

"Toilet's broke," she called, testing him. She waited, imagining the serrated tone he used to correct her English when he was upset. *BrokEN.*

He poked his head into the tiny room.

"Why am I not surprised? What's wrong with it?"

"The flusher. It's not flushing." She wiggled the handle. Water sighed somewhere inside a pipe. It was an old-style squat toilet, a green porcelain basin sunk into the floor. Lou called it "the trough."

He scratched his beard. He'd stopped trimming it, and these days it resembled a storm cloud about to burst. When they'd moved into this place after getting married, he'd taken care to shave every day. He was still teaching kids then, and some found the beard scary. Yumiko didn't care much for it either, but Lou only said, "When I'm around kids again, I'll shave."

She stood up and squeezed him arm, for the correction he had not made. "I'll call Miura-san."

In the kitchen she shuffled through the papers on the bulletin board, mostly take-out menus. Underneath the flier for Tan-tan Men noodle house was the traditional two-year calendar—a housewarming gift from her mother. It was more of an almanac, really, full of symbols Yumiko did not understand. A few dates stood out, printed in burgundy; these her mother had taken care to circle with her own thick red marker. Auspicious days, meant for the events that indicated progress: weddings, job interviews, moves. Even, according to her mother, conception. The calendar had not been turned from its second month.

She finally found the landlord's number between pages of the CoCo Curry menu. Miura-san wasn't phased by her complaint; the building was old, like all the others in Tainohama, and theirs wasn't the first toilet problem.

"Thank you," she said, bowing slightly as she hung up. Lou mimicked her high-pitched formal Japanese and bowed at her from across the room. She smiled, to encourage good humor on his part. But she kept the smile close-lipped; she'd noticed lately that big smiles pulled at her skin in such a way that her eyes almost disappeared. Her eyes were her best feature, the color of weak barley tea, and strikingly light for a Japanese. When they'd first met, Lou had asked if she could really see out of them.

"A worker can come tomorrow to fix it," she said. "It might take a couple of days."

"I hope it's not longer than that. I can only piss out the window for so long."

"If you did, Kobayashi-san probably won't notice," Yumiko said. No matter what the weather, the old woman who lived below them never stepped into her garden without the protection of an umbrella.

But Lou didn't laugh. She saw him catch sight of the exposed calendar, its red circles like imploring eyes. She imagined its voice, a whisper: *Don't you want to know what the lucky days are this month?* Yumiko looked out the window, where the sun was setting behind a network of rooftop antennas. She would not be the one to turn all those pages at once, pinching the months between her fingertips like food gone bad. She especially didn't want to see this, the eighth month, charted out. It marked their two-year wedding anniversary, which they'd celebrated by working late, and the weeklong Obon holiday that began tomorrow, when dead family members were believed to visit the land of the living.

They both had the week off, she from classes at the ceramics studio and he from teaching English, and Yumiko wondered how they would fill the time. Lou had balked at visiting her mom and dad. "All they'll talk about," he'd said, "is when we're going to wave the magic baby wand

and turn them into grandparents. Let's focus on us—on *our* family—this year."

She stared out the window into the mess of electrical wires that sliced up the horizon. There would be a baby soon, she reasoned. He or she was just waiting for the right time to come. Lou's tests had come back showing no problems.

Lou whistled a depressing four-note melody.

"What?" she asked.

"Nothing," he said absently, gathering the scattered menus. He piled them all on top of the calendar, the tendon along his forearm popping out as he strained to pierce the clutter with a tack.

"I have to get to class," he said.

"How does gyoza sound for dinner?" It was a joke; the fried dumplings were the only thing she ever cooked, and almost always in the middle of the night.

He smiled absently. "Do you think you'll ever feel like learning to cook?"

She had never heard him say this. He knew she hated planning meals and grocery shopping, and he felt the same way. They got along fine on takeout. "I don't know," she said.

"It's just that we can't eat out forever, it's not that healthy, and since you only work part-time . . . you know, Mrs. Yoshida teaches a free class in traditional Japanese cooking at the International Center on Sundays."

"I—I'll think about it." How embarrassing, she thought. She would be the only Japanese student in the class!

He leaned in and kissed her cheek. "*Mata, ne.* Love you."

"Say hi to the beer ladies." Lou's last class of the week, Saturday night, was with a group of older housewives whose interest in English was a shallow cover for their real purpose: socializing away from home, where their newly retired husbands lurked underfoot.

"Oh, by the way," he called from the stairwell, "it's brokEN. If the toilet were '*broke*,' that would mean it's completely out of money. Not worth anything."

His footsteps faded. She opened the refrigerator and stared in. She couldn't remember what it was she'd wanted.

HER FIRST MARRIAGE HADN'T WORKED OUT. They'd married out of college, but then he couldn't find a job, and she got pregnant and he still couldn't find work, so they decided she would have an abortion. It wasn't such a big deal. People had abortions all the time; the local clinic took same-day appointments. Afterward you visited a shrine and bought a *jizo*, a small cement figurine representing a soul that had not yet found its way to Earth. The statues stayed in the shrine, lined up like dolls in a department store. The priests blessed them every morning.

Less than a year later, he'd come home from a temp job at a waste disposal plant and dropped the envelope from the travel agent on the table. He was going back to Okinawa, he said. He had family there. She felt many things, among them relief, as if some great disaster had been averted.

THAT NIGHT, YUMIKO WOKE AT 3 A.M. and couldn't get back to sleep. She went to the kitchen. First she chopped vegetables: cabbage, *nira*, green onion, garlic, ginger. She salted the cabbage and set it aside. Getting the dough right took time, and she added the water drop by drop—make it too wet, and the insides fell out. Her mother had told her once that the dough should feel like an earlobe. She poked and rolled and kneaded with her fingertips, palms, the backs of her hands. Sometimes she imagined it *was* an ear she was creating, part of an incomplete sculpture. She pressed the water from the cabbage and laid out small circles of dough upon which she arranged vegetables and morsels of pork with the fastidiousness of a surgeon. Then she folded the skin upon itself, crimped the edges together six times, and dropped the resulting crescent into a pan of hot sesame oil. The scream of the dumpling hitting the oil sometimes woke Lou, but tonight he slept on.

She'd come to the kitchen the night before, and the night before that. Three nights in a row was a first.

It was the season, perhaps. Last year the Obon holidays had been a week of parties, drinking with friends, karaoke and fried treats in the park. The final day, they'd attended a short ceremony at the shrine with her family, honored her dead grandparents by lighting incense, and, as an afterthought, said a prayer for the soul of Yumiko's unborn baby. Afterward she and Lou had met up with friends and danced at a nightclub until the sun came up.

This year, their friends were traveling, or had babies of their own. Her parents had moved back to her mother's hometown in Nagano. Lou had come home from work on edge that night, and they had argued again about how to spend the coming week. If they weren't going to visit her parents, she wanted to do at least a couple of the traditional things she'd grown up doing: joining the crowds along the river, visiting the temple. It was a Japanese holiday, after all. She went along every year to Thanksgiving dinner at the International Center and pretended to like green bean casserole, didn't she?

But Lou had other ideas.

"Can't we go camping or something? Get some peace and quiet and skip the dead-celebrating thing? We don't need to be thinking about the dead this year. Or at least, I don't need to. You seemed to enjoy it fine last year at the shrine."

"Lou. It was never alive."

"What?"

"It's not dead. It was never alive."

He said nothing.

"It's just waiting for the right time. You know that's what we believe."

"I just don't see why you have to rub it in my face every year that someone else got you pregnant and it was just an . . . *inconvenience*."

"A year or two isn't long," she said. "We should be more patient. It isn't easy."

"You made a baby for him easily enough."

She walked out and wandered the streets for over an hour, fuming. Yet she could see his point, and that was what hurt the most. The doctor could find no explanation for their difficulty. She wanted more than anything to be a mother, to bear his child, and no matter what the doctor said to the contrary, she still wondered if her abortion had hurt their chances.

When she returned, his eyes were red. He apologized so sincerely that she gave in and told him they could stay home for the holiday. They went to bed after that, and though it appeared things had been resolved, a gap separated their futon, and they fell asleep before either moved to close the space.

HEAVY POUNDING WOKE YUMIKO the next morning. The door, she realized groggily. She glanced at the clock as she threw on her robe: 8 a.m.

"Mornin'." A chubby man stood in the hall, humming under his breath. He looked inside as if waiting for the man of the house to appear. When he did not, the man shrugged and said, "Here for the toilet," and stepped over the shoes heaped in the entranceway.

Yumiko backed away, rubbing her eyes. "Um—"

"New toilet's going in," he said. "Might be a few days."

"New toilet? I don't believe we . . ."

He stood in his boots, in her kitchen, and looked around.

"Gyoza, yum!" He stalked over to the stove. "Do you mind?" he asked, his hand inches above the plate.

"Oh! Yes, yes, please—eat up."

In the bedroom, Lou was half-awake.

"Let's go out of the house today," she said.

THEY WENT TO THE BEACH. It was uncomfortably warm already, and Lou's hair puffed up in the humidity. They arrived early enough to get a prime spot, but Lou, as always, led her to a rocky corner near the breakwater. He was the kind of man that, given first choice of desserts, would choose the most undesirable one, just so he wouldn't have to share it. He avoided crowds if at all possible. Once, when they'd first met, she'd asked him why he'd settled in such an overpopulated, and foreign, country. "To escape my family," he'd joked, and when she pressed him seriously, he'd finally responded that he enjoyed the challenge. As she bobbed among the waves, studying him in his corner, she reflected that her husband seemed to enjoy a certain *lack* of challenge, as well.

They'd met in one of her introductory ceramics classes. He was thirty-one; she twenty-seven. He was her worst student. It wasn't that he didn't listen; on the contrary, he hung on her every word. But his first project, a pinch pot, fell apart in the kiln, which she hadn't seen happen in years. And the next one, the slab pot, simply wouldn't stay together. Even though he used the exact amount of slurry she prescribed, the final wall wouldn't attach.

One night he stayed after class so she could fix his slab pot. "I've never seen anyone so bad at clay," she teased. "Most people have at least some instinct for it. Humans have been doing this for thousands of years." She tried to show him how to roll a thin coil and lightly press and weld it to the side slabs at the correct angle. He laughed and said, in stumbling Japanese, "I'm much better at eating. Do you want to have dinner?"

They talked all night. Her English had been better than his Japanese, and still was, thanks to the two years after college she'd spent in Chicago, studying sculpture. When it turned out that neither of them actually lived in Tokyo, but an hour east and only four train stops apart, they called it fate. A year later, they got married and moved closer to the seaside, dingy as it was. They wanted their children to grow up smelling the ocean.

The beach did get crowded eventually; the crowd grew to such a size that even their sad patch of sand was not spared, and they drove home. On the ride back, Yumiko found herself hoping that the plumber would still be there, pounding and humming.

WHEN THEY RETURNED, tools littered the kitchen floor so thoroughly there was no way to reach the refrigerator without kicking something. A puddle sat defiantly in the bathroom doorway, and as they stood in silence, a bead of water fell into it with a *plop*!

"You've got to be fucking kidding me," Lou said. He kicked a cigarette butt from the entranceway and began picking his way to the bathroom door.

The only thing more annoying to Lou than smokers were the *bosozoku*, "noise gangs" of teens who removed the mufflers from their motorbikes and raced up and down side streets, shattering the silence at odd hours of the night. Once, last month, when a group had gathered in the parking lot next door, Lou had jumped out of bed and climbed onto the roof with a carton of eggs. After some confusion and yelling, the roar of engines faded. Smiling in the dark, she thought to herself, a Japanese man would never have done that.

"He took out the toilet!" he called.

"Yeah," Yumiko said slowly, "he mentioned putting a new one in."

"You knew about this?"

She shrugged. "Only since the morning. It will take a little longer, but won't it be nice to have a normal, you know . . . king's chair?"

"Throne. It would be nicer to not have my house torn apart."

"Miura-san thinks he was doing something nice for you."

"I don't need a special potty because I'm a *gaijin*."

"It will be nice for me too, recently most places don't use—"

"And he'll expect me to be so grateful," Lou went on, and bowed deeply, throwing his arms out to his sides. "Yes, I'm so indebted to you, I can't use my kitchen, my apartment's flooded, and everything reeks."

"We could go to my parents' home. They really— what?" He was staring at the metal ladder that led to the roof, looking suddenly enlightened.

Slowly, he said, "No. We're definitely staying here."

"You have an idea."

"We'll move onto the roof." He rubbed his hands together. "That's it. It's perfect! We'll bring the futons up, some books, your art stuff, whatever we want. It never rains in August, and it's warm enough to sleep outside. The perfect vacation."

"You are kidding," she said, but he was already inside, throwing open the sliding doors that hid the futon. She looked doubtfully at the ladder, then back into the apartment. On the bulletin board she could see the calendar, its gilded edges poking out beneath the pile of menus. Lou, so obviously pleased, lumbered toward her with an armload of pillows. She reflected on the portability of their lives and the things in it, how even the marital bed was easily hidden away behind doors that slid soundlessly, like ghosts.

SHE WOKE UP STARING INTO the pink-dappled sky. Lou slept facing away from her, his body curled around a pillow. For once, he did not snore.

The air was calm, heavy on her face yet soothingly cool, like a washcloth. She did not move, and breathed only shallowly. She imagined she was floating in a bubble that might pop at any moment.

And then a voice: "Kirei, da ne?"

Beautiful, isn't it?

So he was awake after all. It had taken her a moment to identify Lou's voice—as if it could have been anyone else, up there. But he spoke Japanese with her so rarely these days that other possibilities had entered her mind first. Her ex-husband, for one.

"*Un,*" she acknowledged.

A moment later, he rolled over. "What shall we do today? The beach? An art museum?"

She watched the clouds. The way he put the past behind him amazed her, this capacity for acting like nothing had been, or could ever be, wrong.

"Or maybe . . . hey, how do you say 'rooftop nudist colony' in Japanese?"

She sat up and ran her fingers through the tangled hair that fell halfway down her back. He was in a good mood, at least. "The beach again sounds nice. And we could shower there. My hair is gross."

"I had this dream," he said, reaching up and fingering a lock of her hair. "You had your hair in braids. Have you ever done it that way?"

"When I was in high school, maybe."

He sat up and began to divide her hair into sections. "Did I ever tell you how glad I am you don't dye your hair?"

"All the time."

"I don't know what I'm doing," he said. "Do you just wind it around like this?" He swizzled two pieces together.

"Here." She took the pieces and smoothed them between her hands. "You make three sections. *Ichi, ni, san. Mitsu ami, dan-dan.*" Her fingers moved nimbly as she recited the rhyme. "The boy chases the girl, captures her beneath him, the third comes between, like this, and from then on they are—" she paused, then left off the last line of the grade-school chant, which played on in her head: "a happy family woven together."

"*Jaan*!" she said instead, holding the finished braid out to him like an offering. He took it.

"Amazing how girls can do that to their own hair," he said. "Like it's an instinct or something." He took her hand. "It's our own little world up here. Do you like it?"

She *did* like it. "It's like we're flying on a magic carpet. Or explorers on the frontier."

"My pioneer woman," he said, and lay down, pulling her with him. The sky was brightening; a mile away at the town park the trees on Shiroyama stood silhouetted against it, like sentries keeping a polite distance.

THE SEASIDE WAS NOT AS CROWDED AS USUAL; many people had left town for the holiday. This put Lou in a carefree, happy mood, and when they returned home, hungry and sun-baked, the kitchenful of tools did not dent his good spirits.

They agreed immediately on a restaurant, a ramen place known all over the prefecture for its pork broth, and took a booth in back. Lou filled her in on the beer ladies. Kimiko, a woman of sixty who had climbed Mt. Fuji every year since she was in college, was back after a two-week illness. She'd been bedridden, she told them, and her husband, for the first time in his life, had had to prepare their meals.

"The guy didn't know where to find the toaster," Lou told her. "So he cooked the bread right on the stove burner!"

"Even *I* can make toast," Yumiko said.

"Makes me think maybe I should learn how to cook a few things. We could take a class together."

She loved this enthusiasm. Here was the Lou she'd taught in her pottery class, ready to try anything. "Why not?" she said.

After dinner they walked along the river. On Friday, the boardwalk would be packed with people dancing, drinking, and lighting lanterns; booths squeezed in along the riverside would sell everything from fried squid on a stick to giant pet crickets. But now they were alone on the dark walkway. Even the river seemed motionless, and the only sound they heard was the clacking of the one-car train that brought tourists to and from the seaside. Though it was too late for the beach, the train still ran, shuttling nothing but air.

In the silence, she felt she was expanding, beginning to take up more space in the universe. She wondered if this was what being an adult meant. Over the next few days, she and Lou developed a routine: mornings spent on the beach, the scorching afternoons whiled away at the oddly named Café Sometimes. The café was a lucky find, open during the holiday week and stocked with American board games Yumiko remembered from her days in Chicago: Connect Four, Monopoly, Life. A Grand Opening banner hung above the door. Always the sole customers, they basked in the attention of the owner, who fussed over them as if *they* were the new things.

In the evenings they picnicked on the roof. Yumiko

brought up some clay and created a makeshift studio; the little objects she fashioned by moonlight—cups, saucers, vases—she left out to bake in the next day's sun.

She threw up on Friday night. It came upon her while she was adding water to a batch of gyoza dough, and she barely managed to step over to the sink in time. When she stood back up from the basin, excitement burst through her chest and set her body tingling. She was not one to vomit for nothing. Other than one night of heavy drinking, the last time she'd thrown up was when she was pregnant.

She washed her face with dish soap, rinsed out the sink, and sank to the floor. She breathed deeply, wondering what to do. There was a convenience store nearby where she could buy a pregnancy test. But Lou was due back any minute and would wonder about the half-made dumplings. He'd be sure to ask where she'd gone, and she didn't want to raise his hopes in case it was a false alarm. She had disappointed him enough.

As she rose to continue mixing the dough, she heard him coming up the stairs. A moment later, he opened the door a sliver and spoke through the crack.

"Yumi, come up in five minutes. I have a little surprise for you."

"OK," she replied. The last time he'd said that, he'd asked her to marry him.

She retrieved her makeup kit from the bathroom, which was still crowded with tools and pieces of pipe. The new toilet, complete with heated seat ring and button-activated bidet, sat in the shower, waiting.

In the kitchen, she applied blush, checking her reflection in the toaster. She brushed her hair and drank some water. They both wanted a baby girl. She hurried outside to the ladder, leaving the dough behind.

She had so masterfully avoided discussing the evening's plans that she'd forgotten to think about them herself. Friday, of course, was the final day of Obon, when the spirits returned home, the day of the riverside festival when candlelit paper lanterns crowded the water. Once, as a child, she had seen one of the floating lanterns catch fire. The paper was so thin that the entire lantern seemed to disappear in a single flash. Her father had called it a bad omen. Secretly, though, she had found the sight pleasing, surrounded as it was by such uniformity.

She climbed up the ladder more carefully than she had in previous days. She hoped his surprise wouldn't interfere with a trip down to the river, where they could piece together a meal from the food booths, drink some beer—no, no beer for her—and watch the fireworks.

But when she reached the top, she gasped. Lou sat surrounded by candles, cross-legged, among dishes of food and two bottles of red wine. His head and face were completely shaved.

She took a deep breath, and let her gaze fall on the candles behind him. The flames looked hardened; the air was so still she imagined there was no wind left on the planet; it had blown its last gust and given up.

"The fireworks are starting soon," he said, reaching for her. "We'll have the best view in the city."

"Your hair," she said.

"It got to be too much. So I ducked over to work and plugged in the shaver." He rubbed his shiny head and grinned. "What do you think?"

"It's . . . clean."

He made a face.

"I think we could go down to the river. You know, for the lanterns."

"But we're having such a good time up here in our little settlement."

She looked at all his preparations, tenderness rising in her, but when she thought of the river, she held her ground. "Can we please do the thing I want to do? Isn't it enough that we didn't see my parents?"

"Fuck, Yumi." He took a single soft white mochi ball and hurled it off the roof. He threw another, and another. A tiny splash came from below: one must have landed in Kobayashi-san's koi pond.

"Ehh? What was that?"

Yumiko rushed past Lou, stopping a few feet back from the edge of the roof. Nausea turned her stomach, and she swallowed hard. "It's just us, Kobayashi-san. It was a mistake. I'm very sorry." Had Lou gone crazy?

Yumiko saw the old woman, umbrella in hand, bend down and pick up a mochi ball from the ground. "Hey! My fish can't eat this!"

Horrified but slightly thrilled, Yumiko turned to Lou. He was biting his lips, trying to keep from laughing. Lou picked up the plate of mochi balls and mimed flinging its entire contents into Kobayashi-san's garden. Suddenly Yumiko had to fight laughter, too. "Yes, we accidentally dropped one or two, unfortunately," she called out, using the most formal verb conjugation possible. "We were . . . juggling. Please accept my apology regarding your honorable carp."

"You'll pay for this fish! I'm telling Miura-san that you've been living on the roof."

Yumiko came and sat beside Lou. Kobayashi-san continued ranting in her garden, out of sight. "Her umbrella finally became useful," Yumiko said. They both laughed. He put his arm around her and ate a piece of sushi from a takeout tray.

Yumiko watched her husband. His scalp glinted in the candlelight. She had never realized how irregular the skull was, what imperfections hair concealed. He looked vulnerable.

She was sure she was pregnant. But what if something happened to the baby? What if there were complications? She needed him to tell her that he would love her no matter what. To the west, a small white firework tested the air. *Snap.* "I have a serious question," she said.

He put a hand on her shoulder and gestured at their makeshift bedroom, the space delineated from where they now sat by a row of small pots and vases. "Whatever comes, we'll figure it out. *Itsumo,* always. Our problems are no match for us."

He stood up, held out a hand. "C'mon. Let's go to the river."

THREE SCENARIOS IN WHICH HANA SASAKI GROWS A TAIL
\\\\\\\\\

I.

It is her thirtieth birthday. She wakes alone.

Her right hand reaches around to feel a soft length of hair that wasn't there when she took her bath the night before.

She shuffles to the full-length mirror, cranes her neck. The tail is three inches long and gleams silver with a lavender tinge, one end thin and flyaway, the other thick as rope. It sprouts from the asymmetrical dark button at the base of her spine—what her mother used to call her Hydrangea Mole. Her mother loved hydrangeas, but Hana has always found them a bit over the top. Hana prefers tulips.

She slides her palm beneath the tail and runs her thumb over the strands. Such softness, it's like a baby's rose-petal cheeks. The phone trills; her mother's nasal singsong tells the answering machine to keep a positive outlook; women far older than thirty are marrying nowadays.

Hana steps into the shower. It's too early to call a doctor, and though the tail feels odd, it's not exactly painful, and she can't justify the expense and time of an emergency room visit. Water rolls down her back and soaks the bundle. It is thin, dark gray when wet, and the hair at the base rises out slightly from her back before wilting and following the curve of her bottom. She hesitates, then dabs shampoo into her palm and brings both hands behind her back: lather, rinse—and, why not?—condition. She lets the conditioner sit for three minutes before rinsing with cold water. Cold water closes the hair shaft and makes for a silkier finish. Perhaps later she can braid it, dress it up with ribbon. She will care for it as only she can.

II.

Little Hana has just gotten over the chicken pox. To celebrate, her doting parents take her to the Ueno Zoo to see the red pandas, which their local zoo does not feature.

Hana does not like the Ueno Zoo. It is big, crowded, and the animals look upset. Hana wonders if the angry gorilla pounding at the glass is contagious, like her sickness. Contagious, she knows, means giving something bad to someone else, even if they don't want it. That was how she got those chicken pox, and how she got rid of them. She clings to her mother, whimpering, worried that getting too close to a hideous, wrinkly grandma will make her ugly and old, too.

They leave the zoo. Father even springs for a taxi. As they stand on the street awaiting an available cab, a rat scrambles out of a trash bin and across Hana's red sneakers. The child is inconsolable all the way home, and Father must bribe the taxi driver to bring them the entire way.

The next day, it's just as Hana expects: the pink, skinny, hairless tail sticks out just above the elastic on her underwear. She grits her teeth and summons contagion.

III.

Hana has worked at the Asakusa Station Mister Donuts for three years.

Sometimes, when business is slow, Hana calculates the number of possible destinations a person could attain with just two steps—the step on a train, and the one off. Thirty-five platforms, each servicing two or three lines, each line hitting ten to twenty stops, depending on the time of year, week, and day. But Hana only visits platform 23, where the brown line collects and deposits her daily, to and from the thin-walled apartment she shares with her parents.

In the morning, the faces that place orders are alert, but by evening they sag, as if the population ages as the sun crosses the sky. But the next morning those expectant faces are back, ready for fresh fuel, slightly edited versions of the person they'd been the day before. Does she change, too? She feels no evidence of it. Sometimes she gets the sensation that time has frozen for her only, a glitch in relativity, as if she's observing herself from a great distance.

She arranges a tray of the store's signature donut, a plain cake O with a baked-on handle for dipping in coffee. They have tails, she thinks.

A man in a suit orders four donuts and slides the money over the counter atop a thick envelope. She makes change. When she looks up, he's gone. He's left not only his money, but the envelope too. She picks it up and out spill photographs—of her.

She examines them, sharp corners pricking her palms. In each photo, she stands behind this very counter, wearing this red apron, hair tucked behind her ears as it is now.

She twitches and slaps at her lower back; something has gotten into her waistband—a flea, maybe.

WISHER
\\\\\\\\\\

THROUGH THE FOUNTAIN, Nao had come to feel like a father to the town. He thought himself something of a priest: a hearer of confessions, witness of desires. Buying fish, he pretended not to know about the affair of Shimoto-san's husband, or that little Shungo Saeki longed to be a girl. Only one wisher evaded identification: a woman, her voice like a skipping stone.

Most people just called it Old Castle Park, but as caretaker, he preferred the official name: Shuddering Galaxy Common Zone and Gardens. Rosebushes spiraled out from the central fountain like arms, the work of an idealistic planner after the war. Nao imagined each blossom a star.

He had officially retired from the job years ago but had found himself restless without the routine of a day's work, so a week into his retirement he simply came back, going about the routine that had kept him in motion for so long—tending the roses, sweeping the leaves from the path, scrubbing the fountain, and clearing out the coins from its bottom.

The city warned Nao that they were unable to rehire him—red tape; he was too old to go back on the books—but if he really wanted to work, they could allow him as payment the change people threw into the fountain.

He didn't need the money. He lived alone and drew a modest pension and lived simply, in a small wooden house built so long ago it contained just one electrical outlet. Into the top socket was plugged his half-size refrigerator; the bottom socket sat empty. A tiny red spider sometimes appeared there, which Nao thought lucky. Nao owned a small TV and enjoyed certain weekly dramas enough to pay the NHK subscription fee, but rather than use the vacant socket to power the TV, he unplugged the refrigerator. Nao believed in spiders' rights. He also believed that life offered answers to those who stood still enough to hear them. As a young man in Kyoto, he'd worked as an assistant to a "talk doctor." He became a skilled listener—so skilled that when the doctor passed away, his patients tried to visit with Nao. But Nao couldn't afford rent on the Aoyama office. The business closed, and he left for a quieter place.

EVERY TUESDAY AFTERNOON Nao carried a pair of yellow waders and a push broom to the fountain's stone ledge. Feet snug in the boots, he stepped in, felt the pressure against his shins as the rubber resisted the cold water. When he lowered the broom head, a million tiny bubbles shot to the surface as if spooked. He swept. The broom handle was splintered, but he didn't wear gloves; his palms were calloused and any slivers that managed to pierce the thick layer of skin didn't get far; they stuck out like quills on a porcupine, and felt to him like a therapy.

He'd been able to hear them since the beginning. There were commands: "Make her love me," "Give me a raise"; and questions: "Can I have a new car?" Sometimes the coin clutched in his palm pleaded. Those were the ones that wrung his heart out, the ones that started with "Dear God," or "Please, oh please. . . ."

The wishes came in seasons. In the autumn months, before entrance exams, there arrived a flurry from parents and students. Spring was for love, winter for family, summer for travel. The darkest time was Obon, when the wishes began to sound like confessions, and Nao knew the visiting spirits had come to cast their coins while they had the chance. The wishes of the dead were full of regret.

Nao's favorite coins to hear were the aluminum one-yens, so flimsy their sinking seemed magic. The voices of the one-yens were inevitably those of children, and the will of a child, Nao thought, was like a freshly minted sword. These were the wishes that cut him deepest, and pleased him most. He had long forgotten the ring of intense desire, to want nothing more than a fat, sugared gumball. He visited the hundred-yen shop with a laundry list of trinkets: toy car, rubber stamp, throwaway camera. Things like these he bought and left on the ledge, like offerings.

THOUGH HE COULD NOT PLACE HER VOICE, her coins had appeared every summer: thick, heavy 500-yen pieces, a week before the Obon festival, when spirits were said to cross the river between the living and the dead. The wish was always the same, and to his ears like a mantra: *One more time*. He wondered if it was one of these ancestral ghosts asking for another chance. But there was nothing he could do for ghosts.

He always took this wish to the temple near his home, where he spent his weekends meditating and caring for the temple cats. He also took the extra-dark ones, the voices of pain, though these were few. Those voices usually found the temples on their own.

Of the hundreds of coins he brought home, he made a study of them, cataloguing wishes and wishers the way an amateur gemologist might label rocks. No one lied in a wish. Might this be one way to truth? Along one wall of his house sat six Breem disinfectant canisters Nao had scrubbed out. Each canister had been labeled with a character: Love, Accomplishments, Health, Power, Money, Objects. Once in a while he combined two buckets in a philosophical conclusion: wasn't a wish for an object simply a wish for the money with which to buy it? Wasn't a Money wish also one of Power? Eventually he decided that all were merely subcategories of the first.

NAO WAS CONTENT WITH HIS LIFE, with his work and his television and his weekends at the temple. Though he kept to himself, he was known throughout town and that was enough for him, to be greeted by name, drawing no more attention than a streetlamp.

He had planned to live out the rest of his days this way. But the news came that Old Castle Park was being dug up. The public preferred the newer park on top of the hill. There was nothing to be done; the land had already been sold. After Obon's weeklong celebration, the land would be cleared for a pachinko parlor.

FRIDAY, THE FESTIVAL'S FINAL NIGHT, Nao joined the crowd, wearing a *yukata* of orange and green. The light of colored lanterns was reflected in the river in the castle moat. A late-rising persimmon moon dragged across the sky as if it, too, sought to slow down the night. As Nao greeted an acquaintance from the market, he noticed a boy with wet hair and a dirty yukata run past, a disposable camera attached to his wrist by a plastic yellow loop. The boy stopped to photograph a fire hydrant. Nao smiled. He knew that camera, and the sight of one of his "gifts" in use filled him with joy.

He moved on, took in the park, and felt as if the surroundings were an extension of himself. He became the dirt, the sturdy crabgrass. He drank beer from cans and sake from paper cups. He ate *takoyaki* and savored the hot-cold pucker of crispy batter and garlicky cream sauce on his tongue. The thick, fried air was occasionally cut with the cool smell of the sea. He sensed the vibration of his every atom.

A sharp, crunching sound pulled his eyes to one side, where they fell on the wet-haired boy. The child looked away quite obviously—he had been watching him. To be observed so closely by a child felt a great honor.

Up close, it was clear the boy had some handicap. His ears stuck out like mug handles, and his eyes were drawn far out and up, like a cat's. The river-smell of mud and fish rose from his skin. He held the camera in both hands.

Nao turned away and walked through the crowd, moving from one person to the next, listening to their chatter, the tick-tock of words. It was not often he drank so much.

He recognized the voices of wishers but avoided their faces. Once he saw their eyes, he couldn't unsee them. Instead he looked up and forced himself to contemplate the black sky. That star might not be a star billions of miles away, but a firefly, hovering within arm's reach. Or an asteroid, heading toward Earth from a distant galaxy, its approach unnoticeable. Within minutes, the Earth and everything on it would be nothing but dust.

Dropping his gaze, he found himself looking directly into the boy's camera. The boy jerked his arm to his side, hiding the camera that dangled there.

ON THE DAY OF THE DEMOLITION, Nao sat in meditation at the temple. He was too far away to hear the machines at work, but as the hours progressed, he became aware of a faint wail coming from somewhere—in space maybe, or inside his own head—that grew louder as the day went on, and he came to know that this was the death cry of the fountain, that the structure itself had had a soul apart from the soul-bits imparted by the coins it received. Nao sat in meditation for two straight days while the rubble was cleared from the hill and the piping ripped from the earth beneath it. An orange cat slept curled in his lap.

When it was over he stood, slowly stretching his limbs. He felt as if he'd just awoken from a long sleep, as if the life he'd led until then had been a dream. Without the fountain to maintain, without the coins to shepherd, he was free. The thought filled his empty belly with anxiety.

A woman in a green dress like a sack turned up the dirt path. The way she walked, as if each step were a final destination, was familiar to him. There was a faraway look on her plain, moonlike face, and her hair hung around her chin in messy pieces that suggested an expensive haircut outgrown, a woman gone to seed.

"Such a lovely temple," she said, and her voice rang in his head.

Her coins clanked into the donation box, and she pressed her palms together, squeezed her eyes shut, lips moving prayer. When she finished, she clapped her hands three times and tugged the rope that dangled over the box. The temple bell sang.

Nao spoke. "All these years—I never saw you throw in a coin."

She brushed the hair from her eyes and looked at him closely. "I've always come at odd hours," she said. "I don't sleep much."

Nao stroked the cat in his lap and felt its purr in his fingertips. "Did you get what you wanted? Did you get 'One more time'?"

Her tiny mouth fell open. "How did you know about 'One more time'?"

She held her face in her hands. Nao thought she resembled a paper doll.

She said, "I had a son."

Nao nodded.

"He was not well. He should have been in a special school, but I was too stubborn. He wandered away from the class. There was a river nearby."

"Certain spirits take their leave too early for our liking."

He looked deeply into her, taking in her hair, her ill-fitting dress. It wasn't a shade of green but the very spirit of green—fresh grass, elm leaves, the shy curlicue of a sprout from dirt. He looked at her ears and recalled the boy with the camera, his hair damp and matted, the way his dark eyes followed him, had picked him out of the crowd. He would not tell the mother about this visit. The spirits of children were foolish, weren't they? The boy had snapped a photo, Nao was sure of it, the tiny *click* echoing from then to now.

ASH
\\\\\\\\\

THE YEAR WE LIVED IN JAPAN, the volcano at the edge of town hiccupped, covering everything in six inches of heavy golden dust. The sky turned yellow, with clouds so low they were like ceilings. No one could remember anything like it.

Businesses and schools closed that first day; there was no way to handle the ash, no plows on hand in that tropical city. It was a nuisance, we were told, but not dangerous; children poured outside to play wearing bathing suits and surgical masks. Housewives vacuumed the street. Dust got into the air raid siren, and it blared over the city for the first time since World War II. Our family was freed from obligation—Monte from going into the lab, Alex from a day of second grade, and me from filling time. We steered our bicycles through the fine dust and joined other families making ash angels in the park; we communicated through exclamations and gestures, and in that bizarre world I felt, for the first time in three months, part of something.

I got arrested on the way home from the park. A policeman flagged us down and checked the registration numbers on our bicycles; the name on mine did not match the name on my alien registration card, and I was put in the backseat of a police car while my husband and child stared. Monte kept pointing to the bike and repeating the name of his lab. His voice rose. I watched them get smaller from the backseat, half expecting my husband to chase us on his bicycle.

The police station was dark; the power must have gone out. They sat me at a wobbly card table next to a young, bug-eyed guy who smelled like fried chicken. Five older men looked on, smoking and chatting. Occasionally they laughed. The young guy opened a laptop computer, then typed something and angled the screen toward me. A window popped up:

Why do you steal a bicycle?

The misunderstandings never ended. My fingers flew as I explained.

He read the translation carefully, holding the laptop as if inspecting a scroll. He set it down, grimacing as he typed. *The record of bicycle is not found. Lab worker has no availability today for the confirmation.*

One of the older men flicked his cigarette butt to the ground, put his palms on the table, and shouted, "Why you steal?"

A bored-looking woman arrived in uniform, her black hair still wet from washing. She sat on the other side of me.

When can I go home? I typed to the bug-eyed man.

That is difficult.

Why is it difficult?

Yes, I see. You see, it is not believing you tell the truth. He said something to the woman. They both stood up; she took my wrist. I jerked it away. I yelled, "I didn't steal the goddamn bike!"

Handcuffs. Photographs. Fingerprints. At some point I gave up speaking; no one could understand me. The jail was half an hour away by car, and before I went outside, the woman fastened a leather belt around my waist. A rope hung from it like a leash. She gripped it in her fist and avoided my eyes.

AT THE JAIL I STRIPPED in front of the female guard and put on the clothes she provided, a white T-shirt that read "LET'S ENJOY" and a pair of red sweatpants that barely covered my knees. The guard pointed to my navel ring and said, "Ehh?" When we came out of the changing room, she gestured at her belly to her supervisor.

"You must remove ring in your stomach," the supervisor told me.

"It doesn't come out," I said. "You need special tools."

"*Sou ka*," he said, nodding. "Yes. We find tools. *Renchi*?"

They had me do it myself. The room got crowded. Someone gave my pliers; I watched my hand open them and thought, whose hand is that? I cracked the ring and pulled the jagged metal through my skin. There was some blood. I felt nothing. A bandage was taped over my belly button, and I was led into a cell. Two women slept on the floor atop a thin mat.

I don't think I slept. Early the next morning, food—overcooked rice, pickles, processed meat sticks the color of Pepto-Bismol—arrived through a doggie door. One of my cellmates showed me a banana she kept hidden in the toilet tank, then motioned to her crotch and giggled.

The second day, a man named Ronald Ripples came from the American Embassy. He told me, with a wink, not to make waves. When I didn't laugh, he pointed at his nametag. He told me foreigners weren't necessarily allowed a phone call. Secretly, he took Monte's cell phone number and promised to contact him. He told me I could be held for up to twenty-four days merely on suspicion. After he left, I threw up in the hallway.

Ronald Ripples brought an Elmore Leonard novel. To keep myself distracted, I read it up to the last two pages and stopped, then started again from the beginning. If I let myself imagine Monte and Alex at home, I would break into sobs. There was so much to daily life. Did Monte know that when he dropped Alex off, he needed to bow to the teacher greeting students at the gate? What would he pack him for lunch? Did he know that putting the rice maker on high would burn the rice and make the pot impossible to clean? For the first time in his life, Alex would go to bed without me, without our nightly ritual of warm tea and a book of his choice—these days, we were reading *Charlie and the Chocolate Factory*. Would Monte do the voices the way Alex liked?

The third day, Alex had a Sports Day at school, and I missed it. Alex loved those days, one Saturday a season, when the school held an all-day athletic contest. Each homeroom put forth their fastest sprinters, best kendo fighters, and longest jumpers in a good-natured competition for the school championship. Alex's homeroom had tied for first last time, and his winning the hundred-meter dash had earned him instant acceptance among his new, formerly wary, classmates.

A girl in a cell down the hall yelled out a word I recognized from that first Sports Day: *Fight-o!* Then someone else echoed her, and then the chorus of *Fight-o!* got so loud the guards had to shut off the lights to quiet things down.

On the fourth day, we washed our underwear in a long trough while a man in an ill-fitting suit barked at us, words I was probably lucky not to understand but still longed to; my isolation was complete enough that any inclusion, even in a group scolding, would've been comforting. I wrung water from cotton and fought tears.

The next day I saw the prosecutor, a man with crooked teeth and fluttering nostrils. He looked like the prehistoric fish in Alex's science book. The prosecutor told me that I would be released—after I signed a confession. I remembered what Ronald had told me: "FYI, in Japan, once indicted, 99 percent of defendants are found guilty."

I looked at the paper, covered from top to bottom in tiny, illegible pictograms, and imagined spending months, or years, away from my son. I picked up the pen.

Anything to be out of here, I thought as I signed my name.

"It must be your writing," the interpreter said loudly, pulling the page from under my pen to reveal a second, blank sheet.

"But this is in Japanese," I said.

"You copy what it says."

I stared at the paper, my head on fire. I began copying.

WHEN I GOT OUT, Monte dragged our seventy-three-year-old English-speaking neighbor, Eiko, to a bicycle shop, bought three new bikes, and had her confirm they were properly registered. Alex had an inexhaustible list of questions about jail, and I managed to keep him entertained while glossing over the worst of it. What kind of food did they have in jail? Did I wear stripes? Did they chain a ball to my ankle? At Sports Day he had once again won the hundred-meter dash and also set a record in long jump. He told me about the brick campaign—the volcanic ash was apparently useful for making concrete bricks; everyone was collecting ash. At school they'd handed out rolls of heavy-duty, pale blue plastic bags. Part of the city hall is made of ash, he said proudly, as if he'd built it himself.

People at Monte's lab had heard about my . . . what—my imprisonment? My arrest? My jail time? The phrases all sounded overdramatic. Monte's ex-pat colleagues showed up at the apartment to get the scoop. People I'd said hello to once brought up cavity searches and my menstrual cycle. I went over the story again and again. They'd listen for a while; shake their heads. It would always come back to: *but how could you confess to a crime you didn't commit?* I couldn't do it, they'd say, sitting straighter. No way I'd let them force me; put me in jail, I don't care, I'd call my lawyer in Boston. This Japanese system is bullshit. You can't do that to people, they'd say, unaware of their arrogance, of how lucky they were to be born where they had been, unaware anyone else might ever see things differently, or have the right to.

I stopped seeing people altogether. I started a journal and found excuses to stay in the apartment. I walked to the grocery store, though Monte had attached an extra-large basket to the front of my new bike. I stopped taking walks around the castle ruins in the park and stopped taking pictures of interesting things to show friends back home. When I did go out, I couldn't shake the sensation of being caged. I felt like everyone was watching me. Strangely, this made me bolder. At the grocery store, before checkout, I held open my purse to demonstrate that I had not stolen a single carrot, not one bag of soba noodles. When a flock of children outside a convenience store chattered excitedly at the sight of a *gaijin*— a word even I knew was slang for foreigner—I stopped, dropped my jaw, and spun around asking where the foreigner was. "*Gaijin*?! *Gaijin wa doko*?" I screamed, mock-terror on my face. The children ran.

I began to draw pictures of the jail, of the people there; Monte called them caricatures, but they seemed real enough to me. I dreamed I was hiding in a room with no windows because of something awful I'd done but couldn't recall; a policeman found me, and I pretended to be insane, but he didn't believe it, and when he slammed the door, it disappeared, and I was sealed inside, waiting for him to return, to punish me as I surely deserved.

After ten days of this, Monte started coming home earlier; he suggested dinner and trips to the karaoke parlor; he washed the dishes too roughly and broke glasses; he bought an expensive food processor that stayed in the box. I knew he blamed himself for what had happened. Japan had been a career move for him, a sacrifice for me. He'd finally finished his PhD in chemical engineering and a post-doc invitation like this, at one of the world's most cutting-edge research labs, would give his résumé the boost it needed to secure a good job back home. I, on the other hand, had had to take a year's hiatus from investigative journalism in an election year. It was a sacrifice I'd made my peace with, or so I thought.

After two weeks of my refusals to go out, Monte took up kendo. He'd never expressed any interest in martial arts, but one day he came home with a black mask and a plastic sword. He went to classes every day after work. Sometimes he wore the mask in the house, along with a skirt made out of what looked like ceiling fan blades. Alex thought it was cool; I thought it looked ridiculous.

One night before we turned out the light, he touched my scabbed-over belly button with his sword and said, "I should've stopped it. I should not have uprooted my family to come here." "No," I told him, saying what I was supposed to, "we made this decision as a family." How easy it was to say the right thing, regardless of what was true.

He turned out the light and pulled me to his chest, kissing me harder than usual, kissing with purpose. We hadn't had sex since I'd been released nearly a month ago. His penis remained soft against my stomach, and we died down, and eventually I heard the low wheeze that meant he was asleep. The window was still coated thinly with ash, and I stared at it, scarcely breathing, loneliness on me like a glove.

THE FOLLOWING AFTERNOON I ran into Eiko on the way to the market; she was sweeping ash into a blue bag alongside three other ladies. We had chatted on a few occasions; she'd lived in London and Connecticut before her husband died. She liked to use her English. She asked me to join them, and I couldn't think of a way to say no, so I picked up a broom. The first rain since the ash had fallen was forecast for that night, and people in town were taking the brick campaign very seriously.

After ten minutes the street was nearly spotless, and I wondered why we were still sweeping. We collected so little ash in our pans it hardly seemed worth the time, yet still they swept, these grandmothers and great-grandmothers with their crumbling voices and hunched backs. The huge trash bags with so little inside looked sad.

Afterward, Eiko invited me up for tea. I went. Anything

was better than sitting in the apartment, filling notebooks. She didn't ask how I was doing; instead, she talked about growing up in different cities—her father was a salesman for Sony—and the friends she'd lost touch with.

"After my father died, I worked my way through college as a bar hostess," she said. "It was one of the classier clubs. I'd go home with men sometimes if I liked them." I sat on the overstuffed couch and listened. She stroked her long braids, so gray they looked blue. Somewhere nearby, a police siren wailed. I jumped.

Eiko said, "There's a lot that's unexplainable. When you feel alone, many things become possible. Sometimes they would bring me home to their wives. I liked that. It was like getting membership to an exclusive club."

"You'll be fine," Eiko went on. She leaned forward and kissed my mouth. I closed my eyes. I am in control, I thought. Yes, I can do anything, even things I don't want to do. When I felt her tongue on mine, I opened my eyes.

She said, "Not too bad. But you kiss like a man." Then we were both laughing, so hard I could hardly breathe. Then I was crying, for the first time since my arrest, sobbing into her shoulder; she petted my head and whispered some strange, beautiful syllables over and over, rocking me until the tears ran out and I fell asleep.

THE NEXT DAY I RODE TO SCHOOL with Alex for Open House.

"He seems a bit distracted lately," his teacher said. "Nothing I can put my finger on. I wasn't even sure I should mention it."

"I see."

"He's a wonderful child. You're very lucky."

"I know," I said. "I know."

On the way home we rode past a policeman standing on a corner. His thin mustache reminded me of one of the officers who'd questioned me at the police station. My heart raced. I avoided his eyes and prayed, Please, please don't notice me. I'm not here.

As we approached, he yelled. I closed my eyes, prepared for the barrage.

Then I heard him: "I AM FINE THANK YOU AND YOU?" It was probably the only English phrase he knew, and when I looked up, he was grinning, waving. I did what I always do when I'm waved to—I waved back.

THAT EVENING AS MONTE WAS putting on his kendo getup, I told him I wanted to go to the karaoke place. He looked at me strangely, then shimmied back into his work clothes, probably afraid that if he took time to choose a new outfit, I would change my mind. The three of us rode our bikes across town, Alex darting among pedestrians and leading the way to the gleaming seven-story building of private soundproof rooms.

Alex sang "Twist and Shout," and we pushed the tables aside so we could dance. I couldn't resist "I Fought the Law." Monte, in his voice only a deaf man could love, bellowed "Steppin' Out with My Baby," then "At Last," the first dance at our wedding. He held my hand as Alex took over, singing song after song after song, dancing like a maniac.

The next day was a Saturday. Monte skipped his kendo class, and after Alex left for a friend's house, we got back into bed.

That afternoon I packed all of my journals in a box, the five full notebooks and the one I had just started on the day of the open house. I sent the box to my mother's house in Portland. Alex begged to go back to the karaoke place, so we did. It had been five weeks since the ash had fallen, and the only evidence it had been there at all were the blue bags that neatly lined the sidewalk, ready to be picked up and the ash transformed.

WE RETURNED TO BOSTON later that year, and I fell back into my job, and the year after that, Monte was offered a job leading a CE lab at Northeastern. Alex grew up. He had friends, played soccer; he wanted to be a rock guitarist, a DEA officer, a marine biologist. We talked about Japan less and less, and in time my prison story became nothing more than a tale for dinner parties, evidence that my life had been somehow extraordinary. As for Alex, if he remembered anything, it was probably that one year when he was little we lived in Japan, and once yellow ash had buried the city, and then things were kind of strange, and then they were OK again.

CRAM ISLAND
\\\\\\\\\\

BY NOW, EVERYONE'S GOT A VERSION of the story, telling tall tales of their own run-ins with Room 17, even claiming to be part of our circle that year. But when it comes down to it, no one was there that last day—no one but Nozomi. I like to think that since I knew her well and was part of that short-lived group, my account is the most true, but really, I'm just piecing together what I know with what I imagine. Like working a jigsaw puzzle in the dark.

Nozomi was a wallflower, which is probably why I liked her. To this day I tend to date women who don't stand out, whose accomplishments are the adult equivalent of hers in high school: co-secretary of the English club, runner-up for the science fair—or was it the mile run on Sports Day? In any case, Nozomi was reasonably good at being seventeen. I'd had an on-and-off crush on her since kindergarten, but until that final year of high school, we'd never hung out much. We only got close because I was dating Miho—her best friend.

It was easier that way, though I wonder had I been a little braver, gone for it with Nozomi, if things might have turned out differently.

EVERY DAY AFTER SCHOOL the three of us—Miho, Nozomi, and I—would stock up on candy at Sunkus, maybe buy a vending machine beer to split among us, and ride our bikes out to the edge of town. It was there that the neon of Karaoke Live! rose up between two rice paddies. We always asked for Room 17, and it was usually available to us.

The machine in Room 17 was different, it was made somewhere else; a curled, unrecognizable script ran down the side panel, spelling out instructions, perhaps, or warnings we couldn't read. Not that it mattered: we came to sing, and that particular machine had the best selection of songs. In fact, it seemed to have different songs every time, and was known for oddball old favorites, like Ray Sakamoto's "Dragon Curry" or Kari Kari's "Love Me for the Forever." Nozomi once claimed that it had any song you wanted, if you looked through the book enough times.

The karaoke system had a built-in game that scored your pitch and timing. After each song a cartoon island appeared in the distance. "Cram Island," it was called. The idea was that you were lost at sea and swimming toward land—the better you sang, the closer you got. Sometimes the game would comment on your performance, little animated coconuts yelling "WAAA!" or "HEEE!" or, if you were doing badly, maybe caught up in conversation instead of singing, they'd shout, "BUUU!" There were a couple theories behind the name "Cram Island": I joked that it was a horrible place full of kanji practice sheets and crabby, second-rate teachers so bad they were exiled from regular cram school. Miho was certain it was a misspelling of the English word "clam," though we never did see any shellfish in the game.

Aside from that machine, though, number 17 was like any other room in the place: yellow walls, plastic couches, the stink of fresh cigarettes and stale potpourri in the air. A low table piled with songbooks, mics, and remotes, and a wicker basket that held tambourines and maracas, though we never used those—they were for the old ladies who came in with their masks and kerchiefs to sing *enka*.

We liked that Karaoke Live! was out of the way, that the bike path snaked between those rice paddies. It felt like we'd earned something simply by arriving. On warm nights you could hear the paddy frogs singing, and if you got a room facing east, you couldn't even open the window for all the noise. I remember walking out some nights, my voice hoarse after three or four hours of singing and chatting, and those frogs would still be humming along like an engine. The three of us would get on our bikes and pedal away from the neon into the darkness.

MIHO WAS A CYNIC, which made me one too; she insisted Cram Island wasn't even reachable, that the manufacturer had just added the feature to keep customers coming back. Nozomi, though, wasn't so sure. One day her schoolbag fell off the couch, and I spotted the black and silver strap of her bathing suit. (I'd memorized that strap, of course, during our PE swimming unit earlier in the year.) To tease her, I asked if she was really planning to swim to Cram Island. She blushed and joked she didn't need to worry about getting anywhere close when *I* was around.

Occasionally, amid all the clanging, merry filler music that played between songs, two voices emerged: one high and whispery, the other comically low, like a barbershop bass, which chanted a jumble of syllables we could never make out. It was like one of those ink blot tests: what you heard depended on your state of mind. "His sky crime fell over the land," they sang to me once, and another time, "This crying will end in her hand."

Nozomi went in on her own a lot toward the end, and even started outscoring me on "Bullet Train (to My Heart)." I didn't think about it too much: Miho's mom had started volunteering in the afternoons, leaving behind an empty house and Miho's pink-ruffled bed. Nozomi didn't mind singing alone, she said; she enjoyed it because she could repeat songs without being a bother. Later, kids who were in choir with her at school would say her voice had gotten stronger, that they had noticed. But I think they only noticed afterward, you know?

THERE WAS ONE INCIDENT during those last couple weeks that's never left me. I was walking out of school for lunch with a couple guys from my homeroom, and Nozomi was coming up the path. I prepared to say hi, tell her I'd see her at karaoke later, but just as we got close enough to speak, she veered toward me and leapt, flinging her arms around my neck. I stood frozen for a second until she fell off and stumbled backwards, laughing. "You were supposed to catch me!" she said. My friend Naoki flexed his bicep and said, "Try me next time." She made to jump at him and he crouched, arms extended, but she didn't actually do it. She swatted his hand and turned toward me.

"I didn't know you were gonna do that!" I said, grabbing her shoulders. I was desperate to touch her, desperate to affirm what she'd initiated. *Do it again*, I pleaded silently. *I won't drop you.*

THE WAY I IMAGINE IT—and I've spent a lot of time imagining it—she rides over on her purple bike, schoolbag in the basket, her school blazer knotted around her waist. The frogs are deafening. She does one of her tiny fist-pumps when they tell her Room 17 is available, the news ensuring she won't have to forgo any of her favorite songs. She jogs up the stairs, tapping each step, though the incline is so shallow she could take them two or three at a time. The door with the handwritten "17" in red marker (someone had ripped the placard off and they never replaced it) is wide open. She drops her bag on the couch and punches *31121* on the remote. In fades the familiar scene: a girl walking among falling cherry blossoms. She sings through "Sakura" three or four times, first cross-legged, then while standing up straight to push the air out smoother. After warming up, getting her scores over 90, she really lets it rip, boogeying on the plastic couch and going through all the classics. Sometimes a waitress passes in the hall without seeming to notice. The waitresses in that place were experts at not noticing.

She can tell her voice has grown stronger from all the after-school workouts, and she finds that she's able to hit notes a step or two higher and lower than usual. She sings both parts of the "Ryozenji" duet; she nails the harmony on "Sounds of Silence," a song our English teacher had taught us. She's never sung better; she's in the zone. On the screen, which is taller than she is, cartoon dolphins splash and mermaids play in the surf. Cram Island draws closer.

When it happens, she's singing "Sakura" for the seventh time, and as she hits the final note, her voice clicks into a new, secure place in her throat. She rides the pitch out to its full crescendo, her eyes shut in concentration, her shoulders back and abdominals tight. Then she opens her eyes, and there it is.

The words, "Welcome to Cram Island," scroll slowly across the screen. A simple, five-note melody plays. "It is high time for you to come," whispers the high voice, echoed by the barbershop bass. In unison they chant, "We want you, only you. Don't get lost now. We've been waiting so, so very long . . . you . . . only you . . ."

Palm trees shimmy; there's a light breeze on Cram Island. A coconut wobbles down a sandy slope toward azure water, where smiling fish burst from the surface. Nozomi steps toward the screen, her expression a mix of pride and contentment. Maybe she's brought her bathing suit that day, even worn it under her school uniform. I'd like to think so.

KARAOKE LIVE! CLOSED DOWN right around graduation. The building sat dark during the summer, and kids went there to drink and try to scare themselves. It was still there when I left for college, but by the time I returned home for the semester break at New Year's, it'd been turned into a swanky fitness club, the rice paddies paved into parking lots. For a long time, I thought about where all those frogs went.

You'd think Nozomi's disappearance would've brought Miho and me closer, but it didn't. In fact, after the day Nozomi disappeared, nothing romantic happened between us again. It was an unspoken and mutual extrication. By the end of the year, after the talk had subsided, we each had a new group of friends and shared nothing more than the occasional passing nod in the halls. Nozomi's parents kept up an ongoing, fruitless investigation that even I stopped following once I moved away.

It still haunts me, of course. It's as if some subtle change took place that day that only I perceived. Like wearing this great thick sweater and having someone point out a hole in it. If only she'd left a note, or some sign for us she wanted it this way. But all we know for sure about that day is what they found during closing rounds: an empty room and a persistent melody straight out of a dying music box. *Welcome to Cram Island!* They couldn't figure out how to get the machine off that final screen, so they just unplugged it. I heard when it was plugged back in, it wouldn't turn on. I have a feeling they didn't call up the manufacturer for repairs.

I still have hope that she'll turn up: I'll run into her on the subway, or it'll be her voice on the line when I call to order takeout. Sometimes I even think about trying to hunt down that old karaoke machine—to what end, I don't know. I'm sure it's long gone, though, like so many things. Like those frogs and their babies and their babies' babies, generations of frogs, those relentless singers.

AMOROMETER
\\\\\\\\\\

THE LETTER ARRIVED in a handmade envelope sealed
with red wax. Flipping through the bills and junk mail,
Aya Kawaguchi saw her name penned in perfectly shaped
characters, tore open the seal, and read:

Dear Kawaguchi-sama,

*I feel I must bypass the convention of commenting on the
weather as I begin this letter because a more pressing matter
is probably concerning you, that of my identity and purpose.
I write in the spirit of greatest hope, and am aiming to reach
the Ms. Aya Kawaguchi who was a student of Keio University in 1969. If this is not she, please ignore this letter.*

My name is Shinji Oeda, professor of psychology at Keio from 1960 until my retirement in 1991. From 1969 to 1970, I ran a series of experiments, the goal of which was to design and perfect a device—dubbed the Amorometer—*capable of measuring one's capacity to love. (Amor, of course, being the Latin root of the word "love.")*

In 1969 there were no departmental regulations regarding the debriefing of experimental subjects. I assume you had no understanding of our research, let alone the extraordinary gifts these tests revealed: of all the subjects (439 in total), yours was the highest score in lovingcapacity. In the empathy measure, you scored an astounding 32 points— more than two standard deviations above the mean.

I must come to my point: I would very much like to meet you. As a widower of two years, I have found the companionship available to me (my tomcat and my memories) to be inadequate. The cat is unreliable and cantankerous, the memories often the same.

It may be true that regardless of a man's age, there remains inside him a kernel of youth. As I have aged, my curiosity has not lessened, but has migrated from my brain to my heart. It is not such a bad thing.

With much hope,
Shinji Oeda

*P.S. This letter has taken me many years to write; the hypothetical results of my test on a Cordometer (*cord *the Latin root for "heart,"' or "courage") would likely be dismally low. I urge your quick reply, if possible.*

Aya raised the letter up to the lamp at her desk, revealing the watermark. The thick paper, and the surprising space it created between her fingertips, made her feel somehow important.

She had never been a student at Keio University. Since marrying Hisao all those years ago, she'd hardly visited Tokyo at all.

She ran a fingertip over the seal. She imagined the professor dropping the thick wax onto the envelope's flap and pressing his stamp there. She imagined the wool of his jacket and the creased leather of his shoes as he slipped out of the house, and the long, slim fingers with which he carried the letter to the postbox in his tasteful Tokyo neighborhood. Now that envelope was here, its wax like an exotic fruit, cut with a stranger's name.

A stranger who believed her to be—what had been his word?—*extraordinary.*

She glanced at the clock above the stove. Hisao would be another hour, and dinner was already prepared. There was still some ironing to be done, but it could go another day. She brought the stepstool to the closet and brought down the box with the good stationery.

She set to work:

Dear Oeda-sama,

How nice it was to receive your letter, and quite a surprise! For the record, the rainy season has begun here, but I will spare you the details of the weather since, as you say, our correspondence is a strange one.

She reread her opening, then pulled out a fresh pink sheet and rewrote it, replacing "nice" with "lovely" and "strange" with "most unusual." She continued, *I have not thought of Keio in a long time, and I am delighted that you had the courage to find me.*

She thought a second, then added, *I'd think your readings on the cordometer would be quite high!*

She sat up, aware of Hisao's arrival. After all these years, the ritual of his entry was well-known to her: the yawn of hinges, the slam of the metal door like a detonation, her husband's gravelly call of "I'm home," not to her but to himself. The only missing element was the punctuation of his briefcase hitting the floor.

She tucked the letter in a drawer and sighed. It was just like Emiko had warned her: now that he'd retired, her husband was always underfoot. She'd had the run of the house from six in the morning to six at night for thirty-one years. Hisao was a good man, had provided a home to her and their son, but she never considered she'd have to spend this much *time* with him.

"You're home early," she said, standing to greet him.

"Driving range was packed," Hisao grumbled. "Too many kids. This time of day, kids ought to be in school, or at work."

"Mm," she said. "Would you like dinner now? Or how about a cold drink?"

She glided toward the kitchen as he fell into his blue recliner. For as long as they'd been together, he'd come home from work, collapsed in this chair, requested food or drink. Now, however, he often wasn't tired upon returning, and though he was still drawn by habit to the chair, he no longer looked comfortable there.

SHE PUT THE FINISHING TOUCHES on her letter that night while Hisao slept, ears defended against his own snoring by green foam plugs.

I am flattered that you should recall me and would love to meet you, she wrote, and took another sip from the heavy glass into which she'd poured some of Hisao's good whiskey.

She printed the name "Aya Kawaguchi" at the bottom of the letter, marveling at how much nicer this woman's handwriting was than her own.

HIS SHORT RESPONSE arrived three days later.

I'll open this letter with the weather in my heart, and tell you that the sky is clear and warm, and the quality of light is thick and sweet like honey! I am pleased and surprised (good news does not often come my way these days) that you are in a position to meet me. I could travel to your town, or, if you like, we can meet here in the "neon jungle."

Thick and sweet like honey! Aya smiled, amazed that there were such people in the world. It was time, she thought, that she met them.

SHE TOLD ONLY EMIKO, who'd divorced young and never remarried, about her plans.

"I'm not going to *cheat* on Hisao," Aya said. "I just want to . . . bask. This man thinks I'm extraordinary. I want to know how that feels."

"Oh, shut it! You're a lovely woman."

"Lovely, schmovely. I want to be *extraordinary.*"

Emiko rolled her eyes.

"Besides, the timing of it, with Hisao retired now and Ryo just moved out—it's like a chance to reinvent. See what I've missed."

"What if he's rich and handsome?"

"He could be poor and crazy," Aya said, but did not believe it.

"An *amorometer*! Whoever heard of such a thing? Wonder how I'd score."

"Me too," Aya said, recalling every selfish, unloving act of her lifetime. The time, as a teenager, she'd stolen an umbrella; the gossip sessions with Emiko that often turned catty; the way she'd stopped breastfeeding Ryo after two weeks because she couldn't stand her raw, chapped nipples.

"Exactly—what if he can tell it's not you?"

"I'll come home," she said.

"Only if he's poor and crazy. If he's rich and handsome, stick around."

Their meeting had been set for noon on a Sunday on the top floor of Tokyo Station, in a restaurant famous for its view of the city. Though Shinji had repeated his offer to travel to her small town, Aya had insisted on coming to Tokyo. The person she was hoping to become could not exist in Iida; she could only transform with distance. And though it terrified her to think of herself lost on the streets of an unfamiliar place, she felt certain that once she arrived, she could be anyone she wanted. Anyone she *might have been*, had her life gone differently. She'd read enough books. She felt a long line of Ayas inside of her, ready to be called upon. The thought made her feel like an adventurer, and while Hisao was out golfing, she spent half the morning pawing through her closet, trying on clothes she hadn't worn in years.

"Well, let me know what you find," Emiko said as Aya went out. "And see if he has any single friends."

SHE TOLD HISAO SHE WAS JOINING a string quartet organized by an acquaintance of Emiko's.

"Do you even remember how to play that thing?" he asked from behind his newspaper.

"Of course," she replied, pairing a batch of socks she'd just brought in from the line. "It was practically attached to my hand in high school."

"I see. Are you going to practice now?"

She couldn't tell if he wanted to her to bring out the old viola, or if he was checking to see whether his newspaper reading would be disturbed. "Maybe," she said.

He nodded, mumbling to himself as he read. Then he said, "But in Tokyo? Couldn't you find a group closer to home?"

She continued matching and rolling the socks, never

losing the rhythm of the work. "I don't think so." Then she paused and asked, "Do you think I'm extraordinary?"

He didn't glance up from his paper. "You're lovely, dear."

THE NIGHT BEFORE HER TRIP, she went to her bookshelf. She never left the house without something to read, but her choice this time seemed of real importance. Finally her eyes fell on the dog-eared copy of *Anna Karenina* she had not read since Ryo was a baby. She slipped it from the shelf into her bag. The weight of the story on her shoulder felt significant; this was a long journey and required a long tale, but more than that, she felt the characters themselves would be good company for this other Aya Kawaguchi.

But if anyone's hit by a train while I'm waiting, I'm turning around, Aya thought.

It took her a long time to fall asleep that night, and she woke up twice, certain she had missed her train. At five o'clock she gave up and took a bath. At seven Hisao drove her to the local train station, where she caught a two-car train to Nishiyama, her connection for the Tokyo bullet.

Safely onboard the bullet train, she shifted in her carpeted seat and let *Anna Karenina* fall open to random pages. "There are no customs to which a person cannot grow accustomed, especially if he sees that everyone around him lives in the same way."

"He liked fishing and seemed to take pride in being able to like such a stupid occupation."

She read:

> *Anna hardly knew at times what it was she feared, and what she hoped for. Whether she feared or desired what had happened, or what was going to happen, and exactly what she longed for, she could not have said.*

She looked out the window. She took off her wedding ring, put it back on. The scenery flew by. She found she could relax her eyes and let the images blur together, or she could focus and pick out the elements: futons lolling from windows like tongues, cascades of electrical wiring, a rooftop rice paddy, a Coca-Cola billboard. Each thing was gone, replaced by something new, before there was time to reflect. *No need to think on a train this fast,* she thought. *If I could stay on this train forever, I'd never have to think about anything again, and life would just be an exciting show of what's passing by on the outside.* It was a comforting idea.

STEPPING OFF THE TRAIN was like jumping into a river. She wandered through surging crowds in search of a place to store her viola, the case of which suddenly seemed unnecessarily bulky. *Couldn't I have said I was coming for a book club?* she thought.

So many people. She was struck by the purpose with which all of them seemed to be moving. A ribbon of song caught her ear, and she turned toward a group of musicians performing next to a bank of ticket machines. They were college students, most likely—two violinists and a cellist. She laughed aloud at the coincidence, she arriving with the missing piece to the quartet and no intention of playing it. The tiny girl on cello caught sight of the instrument and tilted her head in an invitation to join them. Aya blushed and hurried past.

With the help of a young man who looked like Hisao in his slimmer days, she located the day storage lockers and stowed the instrument. Then she headed for the escalators.

She wanted to arrive at the restaurant early. She'd read her book, drink some tea to calm her nerves. She looked at her watch: 10:03, one minute later than the last time she'd looked.

The escalator carried her out of the subway and into a multistory mall arranged in circles that reached all the way up to a huge skylight. The sky beyond the glass was gray yet still bright enough to be cheerful. On the seventh floor she spotted a cosmetics store and stepped off the escalator.

After consulting with the heavy-lashed girl behind the counter, who assured her the color was not too suggestive but rather "elegant and age-repelling," she purchased a tube of red lipstick in a shade called "Shhh" that cost as much as a hardback book. The makeup glittered like a ball gown and felt like satin on her lips. This reminded her of bed sheets, and she pushed the thought away. Afterward, in the department store's bathroom, she applied and removed the lipstick four times before reaching a compromise between herself and the other Aya Kawaguchi (who no doubt would have worn "Shhh" without compunction) and blended the shade with her functional chapstick. As a concession for toning down the lipstick, she removed her wedding ring. Then she washed her hands.

At the restaurant, she took a seat along the wall of windows and ordered a pot of tea. A light rain fell over the city, and in response the buildings and roads took on a fresh sheen and the colors of signs and cars brightened.

A moth on the glass caught her eye. It was unlike any moth she'd ever seen, its wings rounded at the top and pointed at the bottom. An indigo spot decorated each orange-rimmed wing.

She shifted uneasily. The spots on its wings made her feel she was being watched. Her mother said that deceased ancestors came to visit disguised as moths, and she didn't want anyone she knew, living or dead, to witness her activity today. She shooed at the insect with her napkin, but it did not move.

She tried to ignore it and focus on *Anna Karenina*, but it was no use. She watched the action in the restaurant instead. The place was beginning to fill up. At eleven-thirty, half an hour early, Shinji Oeda walked in—a dandelion springing from his lapel as promised. He was not as tall as she'd imagined, but his clothes were professionally pressed and fit him well. Emiko would have found him handsome.

But what do *you* think? Aya thought. Good-looking? Yes. His face was wide and mild, with gold-rimmed glasses riding atop a nose so flat it seemed a miracle the glasses stayed up at all. He sat across the restaurant, facing away from her. She admired his observation of table manners despite his lack of company, the way he placed his napkin in his lap immediately and sat straight in his chair, the warm smile with which he greeted the waiter.

She looked back to the moth. Its black, crooked legs moved slightly. A wing angled itself toward her. Abruptly she stood, cupped her hands over the thing, and closed them. She would carry it out into the mall, let its eerie eye-wings rest elsewhere.

The waiter had brought Shinji Oeda a small drink, which he threw back in one gulp, handing the empty glass back to the waiter. Emboldened by his nervous act, Aya walked toward the entrance, and him, the moth cupped in her hands. Its papery wings beat furiously against her palms. She would pass near his table, but since he didn't know what she looked like, she would not be discovered.

As she approached, Aya watched his back, certain he could feel her eyes. His hair was cut very short, in an almost military style, and shimmered silver under the restaurant's low-hanging lamps. His hair was like the rain, she thought.

She passed him, careful to walk neither too fast nor too slow, and went out into the mall. She shook the moth free. It flew toward the skylight. When she returned to the restaurant, she glanced automatically at Shinji Oeda and found his eyes on her.

Aya blushed. There was nothing to do but approach him. As she drew near, he stood, a smile spreading across his face as he took her in. "Oeda-san?" she asked.

"Please, call me Shinji. And you—you are the legendary Aya Kawaguchi." He bowed deeply.

She bowed as well, holding the position so that she might catch her breath. His cologne reminded her of the forest behind her house.

His mouth was large, his smile a deep cradle. Up close, his gentle eyes and flat nose gave him the appearance of a woodblock print. "I saw what you did with that moth," he said, and clasped her hands in his. "This is a great honor."

Embarrassment washed over her. "The honor is mine. And please forget about the moth; it was quite silly of me."

"Forget? Never! I suspected your identity just from that gesture—such a compassionate act, freeing an insect others would ignore, or even worse, kill!"

Aya was unsure what to say to this; luckily the waiter returned and pulled a chair out for her. "A drink, miss?" he asked as they sat.

"Yes, please," she said. "I'll have—" She thought about Anna, and Russian aristocracy.

"Vodka," she said.

The waiter's eyebrows twitched. "Rocks?"

"A few," she said, certain that her order had been inappropriate.

Shinji slapped the table. "Vodka. Who'd have thought?" He grinned. "Make it two."

SHINJI LEANED BACK IN HIS SEAT, his second vodka nearly finished. They had chatted about a number of meaningless topics—the weather, food, and train travel.

"I have to say, I never thought I'd be having a drink— a *vodka*—with Aya Kawaguchi. For so many years you were just a set of data . . . my imagination was forced to extrapolate from there."

Aya did her best to sound well educated. "Life takes all kinds of strange turns," she said, finishing her vodka and enjoying the warmth it brought to her cheeks. "If you let it," she added.

He leaned in and whispered. "Forgive me, but—how is it you never married?"

Aya had managed to sidestep this topic but knew it would come up, and had prepared her answer. "I just never found the right man."

He nodded as if he'd expected as much. "Extraordinary people have extraordinarily hard times."

He went on, "I've wondered for so long . . . I know now that my imagination is a feeble mechanism. You're so different from what I imagined—" She glanced at him. "So much better," he quickly added.

She began to relax. "You haven't told me about your research. I have a right to a debriefing, I think."

"Simply put, we found a way to quantify a person's ability to love. Their potential. It turns out that not all people are capable of loving to the same capacity. The idea was revolutionary." He leaned forward, touched her hand. "Imagine being married to a person whose ability to love—whose lovingcapacity—is far below your own."

As he spoke the word *lovingcapacity*, he tapped out the syllables with two fingers on the place her wedding ring had recently been.

"From their perspective, a person may be loving to their fullest extent," Shinji continued. "However, this isn't good enough for the partner with the higher LC. It will *never* be good enough. This causes the lower-capacity partner to feel inadequate, unappreciated, and their partner feels the same because, to their mind, everyone should love as they do."

"Can't people be made to understand, to accept their differences?"

"Perhaps. But it is very hard for people to truly understand. We have, it turns out, a tremendous blind spot when it comes to being loved."

"And people can't improve?"

"Our research generally showed lovingcapacity to be a fixed and immovable trait, much like eye color or IQ. Of course, when it comes to the mind, one can never be sure."

"I can't believe I did so well," she said, and just then the waiter arrived, balancing two large lunch boxes and a platter of drinks. As he set Aya's box in front her, a glass of cola slid from his tray and crashed onto the table, splashing Aya and dousing her pork cutlet.

The waiter fumbled, apologizing, and promised to bring a new lunch. Aya grimaced at the idea of wasting so much food.

"There's no need," she said, dabbing at her shirt with her napkin. "I'll eat it as it is."

"Please, ma'am—"

"Really. Maybe you could discount the bill a bit instead."

The waiter bowed, his face as red as "Shhh," and hurried away.

Aya took a bite of her cola-flavored cutlet; she was

starving and the vodka had unloosed her appetite. Not bad, she thought. When she looked up, Shinji was looking her, his face shining. His food was untouched.

"Amazing," he said.

"Oh, it's nothing," she said, secretly pleased. "So tell me, what became of your findings?"

"In the autumn of 1970, we lost our funding. The government classified our work as 'unscientific and possibly dangerous.'"

"Dangerous!"

"Some people felt we were meddling in a place science ought not to meddle. A real shame, since long-term research is by far the most robust in fields like this." He made a small motion with his hand, and a minute later two more drinks appeared.

"Well, I've prattled on long enough," he said, raising his glass. "Let's hear about you. From the beginning. What did you study at Keio?"

She clinked her glass to his and took a long sip of her vodka. Aya Kawaguchi was a woman who could hold her liquor. "Literature," she said. "My first love was Soseki."

"*Kokoro*," he replied, naming the author's first novel. As he said it, he placed his hand over his heart. "Maybe that is why your *kokoro* is so big."

"Or maybe my big heart is what drew me to Soseki." She was feeling more and more comfortable, as if lying about her identity had rolled out the red carpet for other untruths to follow.

He sighed and sat back in his chair, smiling. "I've forgotten what it's like to be around a Keio girl. Don't you miss city life?"

He focused on her completely as she spoke, his eyes wide, like a child watching a fireworks display. She felt— interesting. Extraordinary. "Well, college was a wild time," she said, as if admitting something. "I didn't always make it to class, let's just say that."

"Well now, do tell!"

"Oh, no. Well, for one thing there was the band—"

"The marching band?"

"No, a rock band. Punk, really. I was the singer."

"Ah—I played clarinet, myself."

She nodded, slipping inside this invented life like a pair of old pajamas. "We were called Shards of Black, and we wore only white, to be ironic."

While he was laughing, she excused herself and went to the bathroom. Hisao had left a voicemail, a habit he'd acquired recently.

She returned his call, explained to him the significance of the toaster oven sitting on the kitchen counter, what each knob did, and how long to leave the bread inside. He didn't mention her quartet practice, which she found annoying, but when he asked whether she would be home for dinner, his voice stirred pity in her. She imagined him eating burnt toast—plain because he did not know where to locate the butter and jam—and she could not say no.

UPON HER RETURN SHE FOUND Hisao sitting on the kitchen floor, surrounded by a mess of bottles, boxes, and cans.

"What are you doing?"

"Rearranging," he said, examining a box of fish stock.

"*Why*?"

He looked up, irritated. "For greater efficiency."

"You don't even cook."

He shrugged. She stepped over him and picked up the whiskey.

"Since when do you drink?"

"Since now. Why do you seem to think life is over, that it's too late to try new things?"

He motioned at the mess around him. "I *am* trying new things."

A LETTER FROM SHINJI ARRIVED two days later. *He must have mailed it while I was on the train ride back*, Aya thought. In the letter he thanked her for coming to Tokyo and expressed his excitement for their next meeting, the next Sunday in Ueno Park. He closed with a line from *Kokoro*, the Soseki novel they had discussed:

> *Words uttered in passion contain a greater living truth than do those expressing thoughts rationally conceived . . .*

She reread his letters each morning and began the day feeling like a plant just watered.

AUTUMN HAD SET THE TREES in the park aflame, and Aya felt she'd never experienced such richness of color, even in the rural forests of her hometown.

He had bowed to her upon their meeting, a good sign,

she thought, since a hug would have meant something she was not quite ready for. His face searched hers in a way it had not upon their first encounter, like a connoisseur re-evaluating a painting that's been placed in new light. She thought it might be her lipstick: after locking up her viola, she'd applied "Shhh" without blotting it afterward.

His unsure manner disappeared quickly, and Aya wrote it off to nerves. Her suspicion was confirmed when, after just a few minutes of walking, he grabbed her hand. "I want to show you something," he said.

He led her out of the park, through a shopping area, and into a quiet neighborhood of old houses and narrow lanes. "This is my house," he said, and they stopped in the street. "Don't worry," he said, seeing her expression, "I'm not indecent. After all, we hardly know each other!"

She followed him down a narrow path behind the house. He kept glancing back, as if to make sure she was still there. A tiny shed stood in the yard, and when they reached it, he began unlocking it. There were four locks in all.

"Here we are," he said, pushing open the door.

Aya stepped inside the dim little room, which smelled of wet wood and plastic. A large table, which held a device resembling a seismograph, took up most of the space. It was not a room built for company.

"This," he said, throwing out his arm like a magician, "is the amorometer."

The central component of the contraption was a metal case painted red. Inside the case, a needle hung poised over a thick roll of paper. Two leather cuffs, one large, like a belt, and one smaller, the size of a blood-pressure cuff, dangled from the left side of the box. Rising behind the box like a crown was a clothes hanger—also painted red—that had been forced into an awkward heart shape. It looked like something Ryo would have built with scraps from the neighbor's trash.

"I was hoping you'd be willing to, well, provide some new data. A longitudinal study, if you will!" He set his hand lightly on her arm.

"Ah!" She imagined herself cuffed to the device, the evidence of her fakery pouring forth, and shuddered. She sat down.

"Are you all right? Is there something you need?"

"I'm just not—"

"You see," he said, opening and closing a clamp full of tiny metal teeth, "this way I can be sure . . . *we* can be sure . . ."

She thought of her lipstick, and touched a finger to her mouth, as if testing a wall one had regretfully painted.

"I think I should go," she said.

HER TRAIN WASN'T DUE for over an hour. She wandered the fluorescent underground corridors of the station, passing shops advertising souvenirs for places elsewhere—blackened eggs from Hakone, tiny limes from Shikoku, *habu* liquor from Okinawa. She wondered how many of the gifts she'd received over the years had come from places like this. Was everything so false?

She heard the music long before she saw the players;

it came from nearly the same place as the first time, next to the ticket machine for the Hibiya subway line, which, she'd learned from Shinji, was the deepest subway in the world. If you stood at the bottom of the Hibiya escalator, it was said, you could feel the heat of hell and see the light from heaven.

She looked at the spot the quartet-minus-one had been a week before but found it empty. She followed the melody with her ear. It was coming, she realized, from beyond the ticket gates, rising up the escalator.

She made her decision at once; or rather, she reflected later, her heart had made it for her—a luxury she had not allowed herself in many years. Inside the stall of a nearby bathroom, Aya flipped the latches on her viola case. She lifted the instrument from its bed and, drawing the ancient bow across the strings, began to play.

The strings were old; the A and G were frayed along the bowline and she worked the tuning pegs, cradling the wooden body to her chest. Shoes clattered on the disinfected floors, doors slammed, and hands were washed, and for once in her life, Aya did not care who observed her. These women were strangers, yet they shared this city; maybe some had been students at Keio University, maybe the other Aya Kawaguchi was in the stall next to her, pants down. The thought made her laugh, and without realizing what she was doing, she began playing the solo she'd performed her last year of high school, the first movement of Shubert's *Arpeggione*. Heady, she watched her fingers land on the strings, and though the B was falling out of tune already, her rhythm was dead on.

It wasn't perfect, but she felt it was good, and if she practiced, it could be marvelous, better than it had been in school because everything she had lived through would go into the music. She was no longer a girl. Her fears and desires were known and did not bind her. She hit the final notes with this in mind, standing alone in the corner stall of the women's bathroom near the Hibiya Line in Tokyo Station, and when she was finished, a small clap echoed against the tile walls, and a second later more applause joined it. Aya lifted her head. She bowed to no one, then started from the beginning, thinking how the beady-eyed judge had nodded, even smiled, and said: "That was good, but let's hear it again."

ACKNOWLEDGMENTS

Endless gratitude to Jill Meyers and Callie Collins, both incredibly insightful editors, and to the talented staff of A Strange Object.

Thank you to the MacDowell Colony, Devil's Tower National Monument, Jentel Arts, and the Kerouac House for feeding, housing, and otherwise spoiling me rotten so that I could work on these stories. Support from the Wesleyan Writers Conference, Sewanee Writers' Conference, the Squaw Valley Community of Writers, Fishtrap, the San Francisco Foundation, and Intersection for the Arts was also instrumental to the writing of this book.

I'm indebted to the readers and editors of the literary

magazines in which these stories first appeared, in particular Minna Proctor, Richard Mathews, Sunny Woan, and Christine Lee Zilka.

Thanks to Angela MacFarlane and Brian Beckey for their friendship and the Caboose, where many of these stories were written.

Giant thanks to John Evans for reading many ugly drafts and for years of encouragement; my beloved Kristin Kearns for same, plus champagne and hoops and PB stir-fry; to Jo Ann Heydron, Sky Kelsey, Kimiko Kobayashi, Josip Novakovich, and Stuart Dybek; to my family for their unwavering support, and finally, *domo san-kyu* to my 好きな人 Derek Seymour for that one scene, and for being willing to throw eggs at strangers who are keeping me awake, and for much, much more.

ABOUT A STRANGE OBJECT

A Strange Object is a small press and literary collective established in 2012 and based in Austin, Texas. A\SO believes in surprising, wild-hearted fiction, diverse voices, and good design across all platforms. *Three Scenarios in Which Hana Sasaki Grows a Tail* is A Strange Object's first book. Learn more at astrangeobject.com.